Starting Over Again

Alan Kemister

Visit my website at

https://alankemisterauthor.wordpress.com/

Books by Alan Kemister

The Barrettsport Mysteries

A Body in the Sacristy
Tilting at Windmills
The Body on Karli's Beach

Environmental Armageddon

The Souring Seas
Building Houses of Cards
They All Come Tumbling Down
The Road to Environmental Armageddon

Starting Over Again

A Post-Apocalyptic Fantasy

Alan Kemister

Acknowledgements:

I came rather late to writing fiction, making no attempts to take this task seriously until after I retired from a thirty-five-year career as an environmental scientist. Many people helped me shift from the reporting of scientific research to creative writing.

They included participants in theNextBigWriter, an online writing community and workshop and members of two Halifax writing groups, the Evergreen Writers Group and the Bedford Writers Circle.

Without the help of the people in these groups, my first novel might still be an unfinished draft. I've now written and published eight—three **Barrettsport Mysteries**, four books on **the Road to Environmental Armageddon**, my climate change saga, and *Starting Over Again*, my venture into fantasy.

I'm especially grateful to my daughter, Karen, and Bob Cook and Geogina Godfrey, two members of the Evergreen Writers Group, for invaluable input on how I presented this latest story. They left the details to me, but got me started down a much better path than I would have managed on my own.

Finally, I thank Maureen, my loving wife of 51 years, for putting up with the hours I've spent slouching in front of my computer when I should have been doing useful tasks around the house.

Map of Neuvo Britannica

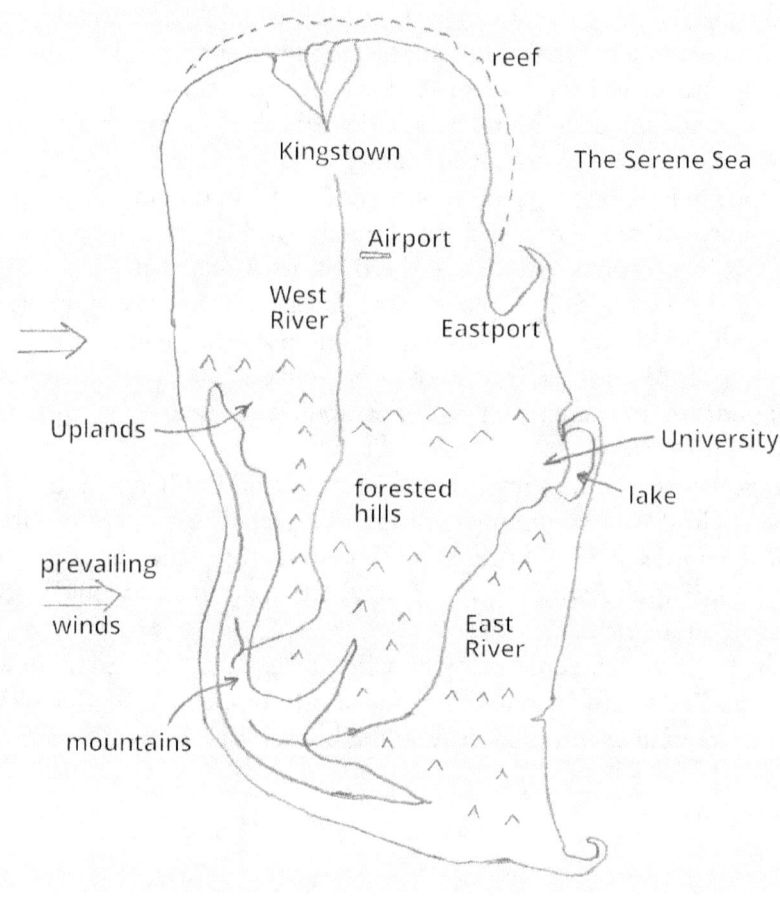

reef

Kingstown

The Serene Sea

Airport

West
River

Eastport

Uplands

University

forested
hills

lake

prevailing

winds

East
River

mountains

1 Intevar's Banishment

Grownup elves develop magical abilities. They can sense the mood of creatures on far-off lands and talk to elves living amongst them. They can cast spells and transform themselves into wild creatures. Fairies have different magical powers. They can fly at incredible speeds and ensure creatures they help move almost as fast. They can also trap nearby objects and pull them in. On special occasions, they can pass on the elves' transforming powers.
Gnomes, let the spirits bless them, have no magical powers.

For a thousand generations, elves, fairies, and gnomes lived in harmony with the animals of our homeland. Then the Apexians arrived on enormous wooden ships.
We reached out to elves on other continents. They said we should not trust the Apexians. They possessed terrible weapons we couldn't defeat.
We retreated from the northern plains to the southern forests, where we can hide and counterattack. For five hundred years, we used our magic to defend our forest lands, never once letting the Apexians know we existed.
That continues to this day. Our magic keeps us safe with the fairies and gnomes in our hidden forests. If we venture into the surrounding forests, we must never let the Apexians see us.

Excerpts from a school book for elflings

"Can you sense the trouble on the distant continents?" Intevar asked Connak, a middle-aged male elf who chafed at their isolated existence. They were friends and comrades since childhood, closer than any blood brothers. Melian, the elfin leader, had transformed them into Apexians when Intevar refused to abide by her wishes. They stood on a ridge above the mountain meadow where their flock grazed. Sylvar, a younger male barely older than a youth, perched on a boulder in the meadow staring at a black box when he should have been overseeing the sheep-herding activities of their shelties. He was a waif Intevar 'adopted' because he possessed technical skills Intevar needed.

Intevar and his two colleagues couldn't override the spells that transformed them into Apexians, but they kept the elfin powers that allowed them to sense danger thousands of kilometres away. After their banishment, they settled into the life of shepherds with a flock of fifty sheep near the hidden forest because Intevar hoped for redemption and a return to the elfin fold. He feared the loss of a visiting fairy, his one link with the hidden forest if they wandered farther away.

He swept his extended arm from the northeast through north and northwest to the west. "I feel it from all those directions. The problem, whatever it is, must be worldwide."

When Connak nodded, Intevar continued. "What's with Melian and her advisors? Can't they sense the trouble?"

Connak's nodding changed to side-to-side headshaking before staring at Intevar. "You know the answer. Melian's a chosen leader, intent on maintaining her popularity. She won't acknowledge a knotty problem until she can't avoid it."

Intevar, a once influential elf, had refused to keep his predictions of an imminent geopolitical disaster to himself. His sister Melian, the leader of the elves, fairies, and gnomes in the hidden forest, grew frustrated with his intransigence. She cast a spell that transformed Intevar and his two disciples into Apexians, members of the marauding apex bipeds, and banished them.

"Bloody stupid attitude," Intevar replied.

"Give her a break. She approved your massive protected forest to preserve the flora and fauna from the calamity you foresee. That's an enormous commitment, but one that won't get her in trouble with her supporters. A policy that involves interaction with the Apexians would."

In his heart, Intevar knew Connak was right. He was just too stubborn and perhaps a little too jealous of his sister's success to admit it.

"So we wait for the turmoil to reach our shores?"

"No choice. Abandoning our long-standing policy of isolation from the Apexians isn't an option."

Intevar stomped down the path to the meadow with his grazing flock. "Not until annihilation hangs over our heads."

Connak chased after him. "That's where we stand. Waiting until all hell breaks loose before we storm the ramparts is risky, but we have no choice?"

"I disagree. I'm counting on Melian to realize she needs our help before we reach that stage. When that happens, we must know what we're facing."

"How will we gather the information we need isolated here in the middle of nowhere?"

"Electronically, like all Apexians."

Connak grabbed Intevar's arm and dragged him to a stop. "I'll follow wherever you lead us, but I'm perplexed. I sure hope you know what you're doing."

Intevar pulled his arm free and continued down the path. When they reached the meadow, Connak stared at the box Sylvar manipulated. It had a screen with text and images, and a panel with Apexian characters. "What's that?" he asked Sylvar.

"Universal Communicator and Knowledge Repository. Apexians use them to follow events all over the planet."

"And you know how to operate it?" Connak asked Intevar. His wide-eyed expression telegraphed his befuddlement with Apexian technology.

"Sylvar does," Intevar replied. "If you watch the sheep, he'll tell us what he's learned."

At Intevar's request, Sylvar began describing the Apexians' view of their planet's two major land masses separated by large oceans.

"The larger continent occupies nearly half of the northern hemisphere, extending from the Tempestuous Ocean in the west to the Serene Sea in the east. The dominant Apexians, nicknamed alphas by most, call the northwestern part 'the Ancestral Lands'."

"North and northwest of us," Connak said. "What's to the east?"

"A second continent that extends from the southern subpolar region to the northern polar waters. It's just as old, but called the NewFoundWorld by the expansionist and egotistical alphas of the Ancestral Lands because they 'discovered' it during their grand age of exploration."

"Where do we fit into this picture?" Connak asked. Sylvar's explanation had clearly sparked his interest.

"Islands dot the tropical and southern temperate waters of the Serene Sea. Most are small, but two meet their definition of subcontinents. Our homeland, Neuvo Britannica to the alphas, is large, and it extends farther south than any other, but it's not of sub-continental proportions."

"Okay, that's the background," Intevar said. Connak needed the geography lesson, but he wanted to focus on the brewing crisis. "What have you learned about the trouble we sense in distant lands?"

"Populations everywhere are concerned about industrial carbon emissions, the polarization of political attitudes, global pandemics, the breakdown in world trade, and the disintegrating global financial order.

Expanding populations and a disparity between fertility in the less and more developed worlds, wealth accumulating in fewer and fewer hands, and the ascendancy of autocratic regimes bent on territorial aggression add to their worries. Governments and global institutions aren't solving these problems."

"Presumably Apexians on Neuvo Britannica share these concerns."

Sylvar nodded. "Nothing suggests a groundswell of opposition to Neuvo Britannica's colonial masters."

Intevar patted Sylvar on the back. "Good start, but we need more. Flesh out your story, make it convincing, and we'll take it to my blinkered sister."

"And how will we manage that?" Connak asked.

Intevar laughed. His compatriots weren't as observant as he hoped. "Aurora, one of Melian's fairies, appears at night. If we have something to say, she'll get word to Haryk, Melian's closest advisor. He'll appear with her response, disguised as an animal. So, count your sheep. If you have fifty-one, the extra one will be Haryk."

2 Ethan Encounters a Bear

Neuvo Britannica is as close as one can get to a utopia hidden away in the southern reaches of the Serene Sea. We have a diverse, fertile, lowland plain that provides eighty per cent of the agricultural products our island needs with large surpluses of many for export. Kingstown, our capital, is an industrial and technological hub. We supply ourselves and the world with innovative products.

South Serene University is near the east coast in the transition between coastal plains and forested hills. We're only fifty kilometres south of Eastport, the island's only commercial port, and a similar distance from the island's International Airport.

The perfect location for a modern undergraduate and graduate school that competes with the world's best.

Excerpt from a South Serene University promotional brochure

A deep-throated growl welcomed Ethan Johnson, a graduate student in biology at Neuvo Britannica's only university, as he opened his apartment door. He'd been deep in thought and oblivious to any unusual developments after spending the evening in the university library, researching the stress response of black bears. A horrible stench preceded an enormous bear emerging from his kitchen. He tried to retreat to the hallway, pulling the door closed behind him, but it wouldn't budge. A strange force propelled him into his flat and slammed the door. His eyes darted from side to side, searching for anything he might use to defend himself. He saw nothing but a sturdy stick he used while walking in the forest.

"Check your computer," the beast said. "It has critical information on coral reefs."

"Wh-who are you?" Ethan stammered as he backed against the door, wielding his walking stick. "Wh-why are you here?"

"I just said. To provide you with critical information on the impacts of global warming on corals."

"But I know nothing about corals. I'm studying bears."

11

It raised one massive paw with extended claws. With one flick of its wrist, Ethan's walking stick skittered across his apartment's floor. The bear bared its teeth. "I'm aware of that. It's why I appeared in this form."

"B-but you're so large. Couldn't you assume a less-threatening form?"

"Like this?" it said, as it transformed into a leering wolf.

"N-not really. How about something less intimidating? A deer, perhaps."

"Such messy creatures, but if you insist," it said as it deposited its calling card on Ethan's carpet.

He drew a deep breath while staring into the big brown eyes of the delicate-looking doe. "Better. Now, what do you want?"

"What's your problem?" the shape-shifting beast replied. Its voice was softer and more feminine, but no less demanding. "Read the stuff we sent you and make sure your pathetic leaders get the message."

"But I'm not studying corals. They won't listen to me."

"Convince them. And don't mess up."

"What if I do?"

The deer transformed into a tiger that leapt without warning. Ethan crumpled to the floor and rolled into a foetal ball. The tiger sailed over his head and disappeared through the closed door.

When he recovered enough to stand on wobbly legs without collapsing, he gazed around his apartment. Nothing, except his walking stick in the corner and the deer droppings on his rug, was out of place. He scooped them up and sealed them in a mason jar. They were the only physical evidence he had. Would they provide an important clue? He stored the jar in his freezer and focused on the bear's demands.

Ethan opened his laptop and checked his inbox. He had two new messages with time stamps only seconds apart. The first was from an unknown source. It had "corals" in the subject line and an attachment, but no message. The second was from Emily Dickson, another graduate student in environmental sciences. She was older than the other grad students because she'd spent several years studying veterinary medicine before shifting into environmental biology. She treated her studies more seriously than her colleagues did. Friday evenings in the campus pub were not her thing. Brown hair she always wore in a ponytail and oversized out-of-fashion glasses hid the fact she was an attractive woman.

She had a question about an assignment for one of their courses. He answered it.

After clicking send, he stared at his first message. His hand shook as he manipulated the mouse. Under normal circumstances, he wouldn't open an attachment from such a dubious source. Ethan laughed. *There's nothing normal about my encounter with the talking beast, and I don't want to repeat the experience.* He opened the document.

It described coral reefs growing on the southeastern part of their coast. Everyone knew about the bleaching and other damage global warming was doing to the coral reefs surrounding the northern part of their island, but no one focused on more southerly corals. The few findings were anomalies, migrants that wouldn't survive the southern region's wintertime temperatures.

Emily was in Professor Filmore's invasive species research group. Was the simultaneous appearance of the emails a coincidence? Or was the strange entity that manifested itself as four different animals telling him to contact her?

The next morning, after he failed to absorb a word during his nine-thirty lecture, he dragged Emily to the coffee kiosk in the biology building atrium. He described the email on his laptop and the intimidating beast that drew his attention to it. He opened the attached file.

"Does it make sense?" he asked as he turned the screen toward her.

"Oh shit," she said, before clamping her hand over her mouth. "Sorry, didn't mean to swear. I received this message several days ago, but I didn't open it. Figured it was a scam." She looked up, sporting a sheepish smile. "I better study it."

He was on his second coffee when she finished scrolling back and forth through his pages of text.

"Something's wrong with this," she said. "Corals are one of many warm-water species that could invade our more southern coastal waters as they warm, but not a major concern." She paused, her brows furrowed, but didn't explain what was bothering her. "We need Professor Filmore's input."

Ethan reached for his laptop. "I'll forward the message."

"Already done it while you were getting another coffee."

He almost reacted angrily to the fact she'd taken advantage of access to his computer to forward the email, but he reined in his temper after reading her message. Sending it to her professor from his computer meant she was on his side and not trying to hide her support. He returned to the fray. "What's wrong with the paper?"

"It's a fake."

"What? It's the proof copy sent to authors. And a respected journal."

She shook her head. "It's a carefully created imitation. The authors' institution is real, but their program doesn't exist."

"What about the authors? Are they students or faculty?"

She held up her phone. "Searching for them. Common enough names, but no published papers by any of them, nor any association I can see with that university."

"But the paper's content? It seems real."

"It does, which is strange. Something I'll work on."

"What else?"

She paused, her eyes once again focused on her phone. "Why did they send their message first to me and then to you? We're not the most obvious recipients."

"They probably sent it to many others."

"I asked around when I received the suspicious email. Neither Dr. Filmore nor anyone else in our research group received it. Marc Lebrun would be the most obvious recipient because he's studying corals, but he didn't get it. He was downright dismissive."

"That climate-change-denying jerk! He's a gun-toting, pickup-truck-driving yahoo from a North Columbian oil-producing country. I wouldn't even ask him."

"Toting guns is illegal, but the rest..." she rolled her eyes toward the ceiling. "I agree. He's an unwelcome outlier. He says he hasn't seen shallow-water corals in his surveys south of Eastport, but Dr. Filmore's unhappy with his work." She paused again. "There's something here, something we must investigate."

"And my bear?"

"Come on Ethan, everyone knows you're a long-haired, granny-glasses-wearing, bicycle-riding throwback to 50 years ago. Where did you get the dope you smoked during breaks from reading in the library? I'm guessing it wasn't from the government's Cannabis store."

"I have my sources. Get's me better shit, and it's cheaper."

"And laced, I bet, with unknown hallucinogenic chemicals."

3 The Bear Returns

Two weeks later, Ethan visited his field site to reassess food sources for the resident bear population. His earlier survey showed better foraging potential than during a comparable study two decades earlier. Not the result he expected. His supervisor suggested another survey.

The path to his study site skirted a ravine. Ethan was striding back to the departmental minivan along the well-known route when the ground collapsed beneath him. He scrambled, trying without success to grab anything that might halt his fall before he landed along with masses of dirt, rocks, and sod on a ledge only three metres below the path. He watched his trusty walking stick tumble down the steep slope to the valley floor twenty metres farther down. When he looked up, he spied a bear leaning its back against a tree clinging to the ledge. It had a very un-bearlike pose. It looked like a giant version of some kid's teddy bear sitting on its rump with its back legs spread out in front, but was much more imposing.

"You're on the wrong track," the bear said without shifting. "Food supply's not the issue. The problem is wildfires and floods. They can wipe out populations in a flash." It stared, fixed on a point beyond Ethan. "How's progress convincing your fellow Apexians to do something?"

"Minimal. Everyone sees corals as a manageable problem. Dredging will keep harbour channels clear if they become a problem. And there's an upside. Ecotourism—scuba divers who want to dive in newly formed coral reefs. I wrote an article for the campus newspaper. Several outside papers picked it up, but it won't help your effort."

The bear nodded its mighty head. Ethan was finding the bear's alpha-like gestures disconcerting. "Saw the article, and I agree, focusing on corals was a mistake. Just like your project here. Problem isn't corals. It's green crabs and tunicates and other vermin of the sea. Which brings me to my reason for today's visit."

"So, you're worried about invasive species. Bears are an invasive species on our southern hemisphere island."

"Bears aren't a problem. They're a solitary, slowly reproducing introduced species. We're omnivorous and don't put undue stress on the ecosystem like rabbits or the troublesome invaders I just mentioned."

Ethan's eyes opened wider. The beast seemed well-informed, so why did it start with a flawed foray into invasive species? *Was it a ploy to bring Emily into the story? Why would it do that?*

He nodded, and the beast continued. "You must continue your journalistic campaign, but focus on specific hazards to the Apexians. They may include pandemics like the never-ending coronavirus problems, susceptibility of coastal structures to storm surges, or fertility problems and endocrine-disrupting chemicals. That will do for now. I'll add others after you work through those three."

"Why those problems?"

The God-damned bear smiled! A smiling bear was enough to make Ethan gag.

"They're ones we can influence, but of course, you won't mention that," it said before transforming into an eagle and spreading its wings.

"What do you mean by 'you can influence'? You talking about the Gaia hypothesis and nature's ability to manipulate its environment?" Ethan asked.

"Gaia, Mother Nature, God... Terminology doesn't matter. Point is we will take charge. Apexians need to get the message." It flapped its wings and lifted off the ledge. "There's a mother bear with two cubs in the vicinity. Watch out for her. Mama bears can be downright ornery." It lowered its head and swooped into the valley.

Ethan's body shook as he scrambled to the cliff top. Encounters with the bear weren't getting any easier. The first thing he saw as he resumed his trek home was his trusty stick lying in the path. He glanced up and saw an eagle perched on an upper branch. He shook his head as he picked up his stick. *Is the shape-shifting beast trying to be friendly?*

Emily waited by the loading bay field parties used when they returned to the university. She helped Ethan unload his van and transport his samples and gear to their proper storage places.

"Lots to tell you," Emily said as he locked the door to his lab. "Dinner at the Ottoman place on the Kingstown Road?"

Ethan nodded. It was nearby and not too expensive. Other students raved about it. He knew nothing about Ottoman cuisine, but crazy adventures were becoming part of his life. Why not try a gastronomical one?

"Learning anything new?" Emily asked after she chose a table.

He shrugged. The bear and his nearly disastrous encounter with the eroding cliff edge were foremost in his thoughts, but he kept them to himself. "Nothing from this survey, but before I wrote my article, I visited the harbours mentioned in our mystery paper. Fisherfolk I talked to claimed they occasionally pulled up small pieces of coral with their crayfish traps. Others said they'd found coral fragments on beaches for at least a decade. I concluded corals are nothing new in that stretch of the island's coast."

"Interesting," she replied before catching the attention of a server. She cleared her throat as their server hurried to fetch their drinks. "Dr. Filmore's lowered the boom on your buddy Lebrun—"

"Not my buddy," Ethan interjected with furrowed brows. She obviously had something she wanted to say, so why was she confusing her narrative with argumentative asides?

"Lebrun either sticks to the research plan they agreed to months ago, or he abandons the joint Environmental Sciences/Engineering program and takes on a strictly engineering project. He's cleaned out his space in our research cluster, so we know what he's chosen."

"What about his mathematical models suggesting our observed ecological trends are random fluctuations?"

"Trashed pseudoscience. No one defends his methods."

Ethan sighed. "Members of university departments may discredit his approach, but the climate change deniers will lap up his results."

When the conversation returned to his activities, Ethan avoided any mention of his second encounter with the bear. After he'd completed his standard survey, but before he encountered the beast, he'd paused, leaned against a tree trunk and smoked a joint. She'd guess he'd toked up before heading home. Further evidence, she'd say, his talking bears were hallucinations.

Better to keep quiet, go home and make another dent in his supply before investigating one of the climate change hazards mentioned by the bear.

At 3 a.m., Ethan leaned back from his keyboard and read the text he'd hammering away at for four hours. He paused, but only momentarily, before adding a title to his thousand-word piece for the campus newspaper—'Decreasing Fertility: Mother Nature's Answer to the Climate Crisis'.

After a few hours' sleep, he reread his essay. It was brilliant. His arguments pivoted seamlessly from facts describing decreasing alphan fertility from endocrine-disrupting chemicals to nature's response. His conclusions based on applications of James Dovecote's Gaia hypothesis had serious implications for their species.

He hadn't mentioned the talking and shapeshifting bear. He couldn't if he wanted to convince scientists and skeptical members of the public. It meant he didn't acknowledge a source. That wasn't ideal, but the bear, if it was real, told him never to mention their conversations.

Asking himself if the bear was real brought him back to Emily's reaction when he mentioned it. Was she right? Were they hallucinations generated by chemically enhanced weed? His only evidence was a jar of deer droppings. Did a neighbourhood deer leave them when it wandered inside his garden apartment after he left his patio door open? Not likely. A deer wouldn't do that, and they were in the middle of the floor right below where the bear/wolf/deer/tiger stood.

Discounting the existence of the beast left him with a problem. If it wasn't real and nature wouldn't force society to deal with climate change, what would his article accomplish? His essay, like the thousands of others documenting global warming's harmful effects, would impress individual readers without influencing their world's political leaders or the captains of industry.

His right forefinger hovered over the delete button as he pondered consigning his article to the trash bin. A mighty roar from outside his apartment shook the walls and rattled the dishes in his cupboards. He hesitated. Was it the bear expressing its opinion, or a looming thunderstorm?

After gazing at the clear sky with pinpricks of light from millions of stars, he pushed submit and sent his piece to the newspaper's editor. He'd produced a stellar story, and the bear had given him two other suggestions to work on. After he completed them, it would be up to the force, supernatural or whatever, generating the shapeshifting bear. And if there was no such force? He shrugged his shoulders. He'd have done his best to stress the need for climate change action. Not much more he could do if their political leaders wouldn't listen. But, hey, he'd established a rapport with Emily, and he had plenty of that juiced-up weed. *But she's several years older than me and too damned serious.*

4
Eavesdropping on a President

Sylvar ran from the crofter's hut he shared with Connak to the meadow where their sheep grazed. He stumbled to a stop as he approached. *Did I see Intevar talking to a sheep?*

Then he remembered what Intevar told him and Connak several months ago. 'If Melian wanted to discuss something with them, she'd send Haryk disguised as a sheep.'

He called out, "Intevar, I've learned something really important."

Intevar immediately turned away from the sheep that quickly melded with the flock.

Sylvar hurried up. "Were you talking to Haryk? He needs to know about this."

Sylvar turned when a sheep butted him from behind. "Well, young Sylvar, what is it I need to know?"

Sylvar stared with his mouth hanging open. A hesitation that annoyed Intevar.

"Pull it together. You know elves can transform into other species."

"B-but," Sylvar replied, "there's no one else here. Why can't he look 'normal'?"

Intevar shook his head. "We haven't seen a single Apexian since we've been here, but you know how important it is to prevent them from learning elves and fairies exist. Just tell us what you've learned."

Sylvar sighed as he sat on a large rock. Intevar leaned on his crook, and Haryk the sheep stared, his brown eyes and sheep ears attentive. "I've been monitoring verbal and written communication between government insiders in the four largest Apexian countries for months. The Novorossiyans are planning an imminent invasion of their western neighbours and the other major powers aren't organizing a coordinated response. It's the scenario Intevar's been warning Melian about for years. It will cause chaos, and soon."

"Sylvar, step back a bit for my sake," Haryk the sheep said. "How can you know this?"

"An Apexian's universal communicator. I have one and endless time on this spirit-forsaken mountainside. The technology fascinates me, and

I've learned how to focus on the communications that interest us. They've protected the communications from Apexian eavesdropping, but they know nothing about our magic. Circumventing the protection was child's play."

Intevar listened intently as Sylvar described details of his magical eavesdropping. *This is just what I need to convince my damned sister she was wrong about my warnings. If we can convince Haryk, we're home free.*

"So, Haryk, how do we convince Melian the President of Novorussiya seems intent on taking over the world?"

"I'll summon Aurora," Haryk said, and Aurora, one of the hidden forest fairies, appeared almost immediately. "She'll pass your request to Melian, and we'll give her a few hours to digest your message. Then we'll proceed to the main portal to the hidden forest. Hopefully, Melian will let you enter."

Aurora flew away, and Haryk turned to Sylvar. "While we wait, I'd like to see your magic device and learn how it works."

When they approached their two crofter's huts, Intevar sent Connak off to mind their sheep and Sylar entered the one he shared with Connak. He returned with the device.

"It works better out here because it needs sunlight to power it, and the signals are stronger outside the stone walls of the hut." He described the device and showed Haryk the sort of information he could extract from it. He finished by saying, "Melian gave it to me before I followed Intevar into exile. She told me to learn what I could about modern Apexian society and any threats they might pose. I think I've accomplished my task."

"Did she tell you how she got it?" Haryk asked.

Sylvar shook his head. "You must ask her."

Haryk gazed at the sky. The sun had passed its zenith and was slowly progressing to the western horizon. "We best be going."

"One last thing," Sylvar said as they prepared to leave. "The device may not work inside the hidden forest because it relies on signals transmitted through the atmosphere. The magic that protects the forest may disrupt them."

Haryk shrugged. "We'll worry about that when we get there."

Melian waited outside the main portal to the hidden forest with a frolic of fairies flying above her. She listened patiently as Sylvar described the capabilities of his communicator and his latest insights. After showing what it could do to first Intevar and then Haryk, his pitch was getting quite smooth.

"So it won't work inside our realm," Melian said when he ended his spiel. "Explains why I couldn't get anything useful from it."

She gestured to Haryk, and they moved a few metres to the side. "Do you trust the information he's collecting? Is it time to act?"

"I think so. Find the ones we've identified as new residents of the area of forest we've protected for the animals and Apexians. Unleash your fairies with instructions to instil in them the need to move to the refuge. Remind the fairies they mustn't make themselves known. If our action is a little premature, we've risked nothing."

"And the ones we've identified for entry into the hidden forest?"

"Bit trickier because we don't want to play our hand until the outcome is clear. Then the fairies can whisk them on their way without worrying about showing themselves."

Melian paused, thinking through the logistics of Haryk's proposal. "Fine, I'll instruct the fairies to proceed as you've described. Intevar, Connak, and Sylvar are bigger problems. Obviously, Sylvar needs to stay outside if he's to monitor the situation, and Intevar represents a problem I'm unwilling to address at the moment."

"Send them back to their sheep. Sylvar can monitor activities in the far-off continents and Connak can observe the Apexians we invite into our forest refuge."

Melian sighed. "Haryk, you have a hard heart. Life can't be easy living in mountainside crofter's cottages and looking after a flock of sheep."

"Heart's no harder than yours," Haryk replied. "A while ago, banishing your brother was something we had to do. Now, tracking developments is a major priority."

5 Encounters of a Different Sort

For months, Ethan Johnson collected data for his research project and wrote increasingly forceful articles for the media. The articles used insights provided by the shapeshifting bear to argue for immediate action on climate change. His thesis project was chugging along, but he hadn't convinced governments they should take climate change seriously.

He'd also quit trying to convince Emily his interactions with the beast were real, not figments of his imagination triggered by hallucinogenic drugs. The bear didn't help. It refused to show its ugly mug anytime Emily accompanied him to his field site.

Alone, he entered the woods for another survey. His stride was less sprightly than usual. He and Emily had drifted apart, and he hadn't seen the bear for several visits. He wasn't willing to say he missed the bear more than he missed Emily, but it was true.

Ethan finished his survey and sat with his back against a red pine, planning to roll a joint. He hadn't extracted his bag of weed from his knapsack when a different apparition appeared. She was pretty in a muted way, and from her small breasts, clearly female. She hovered, a fairy, or a similar small winged creature from mythology who was almost a metre tall, with brown hair and glittering turquoise wings. Her long, flowing, translucent dress matched the colour of her wings.

After interacting with a talking, shapeshifting bear for eighteen months, he was ready to accept the existence of mythological creatures. He looked up, waiting for her to speak, but he wasn't ready for her message. "Time is short. The end is only hours away. We must be underground before the chaos you've predicted engulfs your world." She flew deeper into the woods before turning. "Follow me, and quickly! Your life depends on it."

He hoisted his pack and followed. Her brisk pace prevented conversation, and her progress above the forest's undergrowth was easier than his. She hovered when he fell behind and waited for him to catch up before resuming her pace. Finally, the undergrowth in the more mature forests southwest of the university thinned. He kept up with her more easily.

They continued for hours without encountering a road or any sign of alphan habitation. He didn't know where they were when she dropped to the ground by a cliff near the base of the far-off southern mountains. A portal opened, and she charged ahead with long loping strides augmented by synchronized beats from her wings. He sighed, took a deep breath and followed at a pace that was only slightly slower than the one they'd maintained for hours. A glow emanating from her skirts lit his way. If he fell behind, he'd lose his way in a labyrinth of coal-black passageways.

They arrived at a hidden forest, and Ethan's guide approached a slender member of a taller bipedal species with pointed ears and no wings. He wasn't sure, but Ethan thought she was probably a female elf. "Ah, Aurora," she said, "I see you've made it home with your charge. Now, when Dela arrives, we can close the barrier."

She turned to Ethan. "I'm Melian, elfin chief and the leader of the elves and fairies in our hidden forest. And you are Ethan Johnson, a good man and a staunch advocate for environmental responsibility. How much has Aurora told you about our predicament?"

Ethan hesitated, wondering how he should address her. His best bet was to err on the side of excess formality. "Almost nothing, your highness. Aurora's chief concern was speed."

Melian nodded. "And rightly so, the crisis came upon us more quickly than we expected. You must be hungry. Follow Aurora. She'll see you're fed and explain everything. I must learn why Dela and her charge haven't arrived."

They settled in a small forest clearing where elves of both sexes congregated on the ground, and fairies in the lowest branches of the surrounding trees. The sing-song voices of the fairies produced a soothing form of background music. A female elf approached with a bowl of food for Ethan. He didn't recognize it, but when he tasted it, he decided it was quite delightful, with enticing aromas and flavours and just enough substance to make it more like stew than soup. No meat, but that didn't surprise him. These slender creatures were probably vegetarians.

"When the environmental problems reached crisis proportions, we collected animals of all sorts in an isolated forest we created for just this purpose," Aurora said from a branch a metre from Ethan's head.

"Like Noah and his ark," Ethan replied.

"More realistic. The forests, meadows, and grasslands are large. We have lakes and streams, and temperatures that range from subtropical to northern temperate. We can accommodate large numbers of animals in

23

ecological niches that closely resemble where they lived on the outside. Important because this isolated habitat could be their home for decades."

"And bipedal apes? Where do we come in?"

"Apexians caused the crisis, so we felt no need to protect them. We've rescued those who made extraordinary efforts to save the environment."

Ethan stared at his empty bowl. It was good, in fact, so good he decided he could handle another. The elf reappeared with another steaming bowlful without him saying anything. "Thank you," he said before turning to his fairy hostess. "Is this area separate from the animal world you've been describing?"

"Not completely isolated, but separate. We call this one the hidden forest. It's the habitat for our population of fairies, elves, and gnomes."

"Does that mean I must join the animals in the larger area you're protecting?"

"Unless you transform into a gnome for the duration of your stay."

"Transform into a gnome? Could I, like, do that?"

"Not entirely simple, but if you're pure of spirit and follow the proper ritual, you can accomplish it. Then you could join the gnomes, elves, and fairies in our quest to reclaim the world."

Ethan gazed about. He saw no gnomes, and the elves and fairies appeared to be ignoring them. "Where are the gnomes?" he asked.

"Gnomes are shy creatures, but if you decide to join them, I'll make the introductions."

Ethan shook his head. "First things first. I must understand the crisis that caused our mad dash into your world hidden behind impenetrable mountains." She hadn't exactly described their hidden forest using those words, but it was the only explanation that made sense—a forest surrounded by mountains that was only accessible via hidden tunnels through the mountains.

"Environmental degradation," she said, bringing Ethan back to the present.

"Don't you mean climate change?"

"Climate change and many other critical forms of environmental degradation. It has recently reached a point of no return. You must know this."

"I understand tipping points, but I see no need for speed. The non-reversible changes after we reach a tipping point will develop slowly. We shouldn't see the sort of spiralling degradation you're suggesting for decades."

24

"Perhaps, but the leaders of several of your major powers, ones with nuclear arsenals, saw opportunities for regional, or even world, domination. They caught us by surprise in the last twenty-four hours. Hence our need for speed."

"Attacks with short range tactical nukes? Which countries? How many areas?"

"At least four regions spread around the world, perhaps more. We didn't wait for the details. We had contingency plans for such an event and instituted them..." Aurora gazed around the small opening in the forest. "And now you're here with us."

Ethan placed his second empty bowl beside the stump he was sitting on. "Just me. I see no others like me."

"We have many forest glades like this one. We'll keep our guests separate until they decide. Are you ready to meet the patriarch of our gnomish community?"

6 Assessing Their New Reality

After leaving Ethan in Aurora's capable hands, Melian returned to the portal. Dela departed three days earlier to hurry Emily Dickson on her way to the animal refuge. Dela hadn't returned to the hidden forest and Emily hadn't appeared in the refuge. Melian's elfin intuition said they'd soon arrive.

Dela and three other fairies appeared many hours later. They had someone wrapped in silk suspended below them.

"Emily Dickson," Dela said, pointing at the silken cocoon as they lowered it to the ground. "I couldn't locate her until today. She was floating, mostly submerged in a pond and breathing through a bamboo tube. After I lifted her from the water, I realized she was delirious and in terrible shape. We need Iridessa to return her to health."

Melian sighed with relief. "Thank the spirits. I thought we'd lost both of you. You know where to take her."

Dela nodded and the four fairies rose with their burden tethered much more closely because the ceiling in the passage was rather close. Melian followed, after checking the portal was closed.

In a small cavern protected by an invisibility spell, Iridessa waited for her patient. Dela and her three helpers laid Emily on a bed and withdrew. Iridessa, the hidden forest's herbalist and general healer, cut away the silken threads encasing her patient.

She started the treatment of her now conscious patient with the compresses Dela placed over Emily's eyes. She moved to a position above Emily's head before removing them.

"What can you see?" Dela asked.

"White light and fuzzy outlines of a cave-like space. No details."

Iridessa waved her hand in front of Emily's eyes. "What now?"

"Something moving in front of my face. Can't say what."

"Very good," Iridessa replied, "better than I hoped. I'll prepare a medication that should return your vision to normal. While I'm doing that, you can remove your wet clothes."

Iridessa returned with fresh compresses for Emily's eyes and a poultice she spread liberally on scalded parts of Emily's skin. She handed Emily a plain white shift made of extremely soft material and asked her to lie back. "Now, I'll put these compresses on your eyes, and you'll go to sleep. When next you wake, you'll feel much better."

"But I'd rather stay awake. If I fall asleep, I have the worst nightmares."

Iridessa sighed. "Trust me, it's necessary. Without the medicated compresses, you may never regain your sight. Now sleep. It's what you need."

Within minutes, Iridessa called to Dela and her three compatriots. They carried Emily and her cast-off clothes through a series of passageways to a cavern in the remotest reaches of the cave system where the Apexians in the animal forest had established their refuge.

The next morning, Sylvar rushed into Intevar's hut, insisting he send a message to Melian. "What about your bloody sheep?" Intevar asked.

"Connak's with them. I've been monitoring the chatter on my communicator, as instructed."

"So?" Intevar said when Sylvar paused.

"It's stopped. Nothing. Not a word anywhere."

"You're sure it's working?"

Sylvar shifted from one foot to the other. "It's working. I know it is. I can access the knowledge repository, but not the communicator."

"Come with me," a high-pitched, melodic female voice said from outside the hut.

"That's your cue," Intevar said. "You better get going, and take your damned device." Seconds later, he laughed when he heard Sylvar scrambling around the hut he shared with Connak, collecting his belongings. He shouldn't have been so hard on Sylvar, but the waiting was getting impossibly difficult.

Outside the hut, Aurora lifted off and headed uphill from their sheep pasture. The terrain became rockier with sparse vegetation. As he struggled ever upward, Sylvar decided it might be adequate land for goats, but useless for grazing their sheep. He breathed easier when the ground levelled off to an upland plateau with grass and shrubs but no trees. It was about fifty metres wide and several hundred long. He stopped to gaze at the unexpected quirk of nature and lost sight of Aurora. She reappeared and beckoned. He hurried over, hoping to avoid annoying the fairy that was obviously a favourite of Melian's.

When he arrived, he found Melian and Haryk, both in Elfin form, gazing at a communication device that closely resembled his.

Melian handed her communicator to Haryk and turned her attention to Sylvar. "We reconfigured the shield protecting our forest from prying eyes to leave this ledge on the outside, and now you tell us the signals have stopped."

"So it would seem. I lost the channels I'd been following in the four largest countries over just two days, and when I opened up my searches to all traffic, there was none. I can only see two possibilities. First, the mechanisms that allow them to transmit these signals through the atmosphere have broken down, or second, calamities in one country after another have shut down their transmissions."

"The latter, I think," Melian said, turning to Haryk. "That would be consistent with observations in the northern half of our homeland."

Haryk nodded before adding, "and the fires in the southern half."

Melian turned back to Sylvar. "You warned us a few days ago of imminent danger. Did you learn anything else before communication broke down?"

"The Novorussiyans were moving ahead with their plans, and Cathay, the Holy Roman Federation, and the North Columbian Union were coordinating efforts to oppose them. The traffic seemed increasingly frantic just before it stopped."

Melian and Haryk moved a few metres away for a private consultation. Haryk returned without Melian. "So, young Sylvar, you've confirmed our worst fears. We need you to continue monitoring your communicator for new signals. If you hear anything, no matter its content, you must inform us without delay. Got that?"

"Yes, sir."

"And keep mining your knowledge repository for anything that may help us understand what's happening."

"It won't be updating."

"Doesn't matter. Keep looking for insights."

Haryk returned to the hidden forest, and Sylvar began picking his way down the mountainside to their sheep grazing far below. He wasn't sure he could find the route Aurora had him follow on the way up, but at least his destination was visible much of the time. A few false turns were something he'd have to accept.

7 Emily's Story

A few days earlier, Emily Dickson woke from horrible dreams. In them she saw strange shimmering lights all across the northern horizon. She'd looked through her north-facing bedroom window and there they were—actual lights—not dreams. Those lights were the proof they were at the breaking point. Armageddon, to use her father, the firebrand minister's words, was upon them. She had to warn Ethan, get him to use his links to the media to issue a final warning.

As the sun rose, she'd inhaled a quick breakfast and rushed to find Ethan. She hoped to catch him on the campus, but if not, she'd follow him to his forested study site southwest of the university. After hours of frantic searching, she collapsed, exhausted, and fell into a fitful sleep.

A deafening roar and the sight of a mushroom cloud high in the sky toward far-off Kingstown, the capital of Neuvo Britannica on the coastal plain near the mouth of the West River, woke her. Closer, she heard and smelled an approaching forest fire. The heat increased as she ran from the approaching flames.

She'd found a pond fed by a swiftly flowing stream. It appeared deep. She'd used her trusty pocket knife to sever a half-metre-long cane from a clump of bamboo. "Hollow," she said after blowing through it. She gave a silent prayer to the importers who brought this invasive species to their island and waded with her breathing tube into the pond until she was up to her neck. Here, she'd wait out the rapidly approaching fire, hoping the water entering the pond would protect her. During the next ten or twelve hours, she drifted in and out of consciousness as the fires raged on.

Now, she was awake for real, lying on hard ground. It was pitch black. When she stirred, reaching out to explore her surroundings, someone very close by said, "Ah, you're awake again. Lucid this time? Or still trapped in your nightmares?"

Emily refrained from answering the questions because she had no answers. Instead, she asked, "Where am I?"

"In a cave somewhere in the southern third of Neuvo Britannia, but we don't know where. Twenty-four adults and ten children. We arrived three and four days ago, none know how we got here. You arrived two days later. You've been in and out of consciousness, tormented by horrible dreams. So I ask again. Are you lucid now? Ready to join us?"

Emily struggled to sit. She felt so many aches and pains she wasn't sure she'd succeed, but they were preferable to nightmares that were temporarily at bay. She nodded and stood, wobbling at first, but steadying after a few moments. The woman reached out and removed a cloth and compresses that covered her eyes. Light entering from a passage defined the extent of the dimly lit cavern.

"Sorry about the blindfold," the woman said. "But you arrived with these compresses covering your eyes. You kept rubbing them, so we added the headband to keep you from damaging your eyes. My name's Joan Jessup, and we know your name from your university ID. Come, we'll meet the others."

"May I see the compresses?" Emily asked. Joan handed them over and strolled away. Emily inspected the compresses when they reached the larger outermost chamber, one with better light. It was daylight, but a fire burned in a pit at the entrance. "May I keep them?"

Joan nodded. "Come, everyone, and meet our latest arrival. She must have interesting things to tell us."

Over the next hour, as others came and went, Emily sat on a large stone outside the entrance and related what she knew about her journey from the university. The interruptions seemed endless, but information gleaned from the interjections clarified the time line. Emily saw the strange lights before dawn on Monday morning. Others saw the lights in the darkest hours from Sunday night to Monday morning, but no one took them seriously.

Shimmering lights known as Southern Borealis were common enough at their latitude, but seldom seen in summer and always to the south. She saw these lights above the northern horizon, which made more sense because it was winter in the north. But then, how could they see lights, no matter how high in the sky over the north pole when they were deep in the southern hemisphere? Physics was not Emily's forte, but she thought it was impossible to see light from the Northern Borealis south of 45° north. How could she explain Borealis-like lights south of the equator?

Another revelation was equally incomprehensible. No one else saw the mushroom cloud above Kingstown on Monday afternoon. If they all trekked to this forest refuge arriving from Monday afternoon until Tuesday, why didn't they see the mushroom cloud?

Joan said Emily appeared in the cavern deep in the cave system on Wednesday, and it was now Friday. She had over three days she couldn't account for. The timeline had another discrepancy. The others said they covered vast distances, mostly on foot, carrying possessions and often small children. Their various journeys took them less than twenty-four hours at incomprehensible speeds for heavily laden foot traffic.

She was sitting alone, enjoying her first meal in ninety-six hours, a bowl of stew made from root vegetables and a gamey white meat when a middle-aged adult male she'd seen at her grilling approached her.

"Hi. I'm Don Grant, science and environment editor at Kingstown's largest media outlet," he said. "I gather you knew Ethan Johnson."

"Yeah. Friends and colleagues who spent hours discussing the environmental issues his articles dissected."

"More than friends?"

"What sort of question is that? Just friends, both interested in the environment. In fact, we had a falling out because he insisted he was getting messages from Mother Nature. When things went pear-shaped, I was looking for him. I wanted to apologize, admit I was wrong about the severity of the situation."

"Because you saw light glowing to the north?"

"I realized some aspects of Ethan's rise as an environmental crusader defied logical explanation. I had to accept the messages he was getting from a bear were real. Everything was coming rapidly to a head."

Don's eyebrows shot up. "I never heard about a bear, but I agree. Some of his stories stretched his credibility, but they were so compelling, we ran them all."

Emily realized that after four days in a comatose state, two hours up and about left her exhausted. "So, where is this taking us?"

"We both agree there's something inexplicable, something that demands investigation. I propose, in the absence of Ethan, that you and I investigate it."

"What? The explosions, the atomic bombs, the forest fires, all the chaos?"

"No. How two dozen saved from the chaos ended up here."

"But not Ethan," Emily said before stifling a sob. She didn't love Ethan, she never had, but she owed him an apology because she'd doubted him. She left to find somewhere she could rest. Then she could, alone or with Don Grant's help, try to make amends.

8 Assembling the Pieces

After another extended sleep, Emily searched for Joan Jessop. When Emily found her, she posed a simple question. "How can I help this tiny community survive?"

"Depends on your skills," Joan replied.

"Trained as a vet, but more recently, I've been studying invasive species along our coastline."

"Follow me. We have a herd of sheep with some health issues. The crotchety old shepherd who minds them thinks his darlings are just a little stressed. A more scientific assessment could be useful. And our chickens and goats…Having someone looking after their health sounds like the job for you."

"Long as you don't expect me to live in some crofter's hut, kilometres from everyone else."

Joan laughed. "The old guy, Noah MacGregor, lives in a hut and only leaves it to mind his flock. He and two others, Rory and Harris, along with several shelties, mind the sheep. Rory's middle-aged, so could be Noah's brother or son. Harris is too young, hardly more than a boy. He may be a grandson or a more distant relative."

"Were they living on this mountainside before you arrived?"

Joan nodded. "Noah hasn't visited us, but the others, looking for companionship and a little beer, have been here. They'll be back."

More likely, single women who might be interested in becoming crofters' wives, Emily thought as she went to visit the enclosures the refugees had for their chickens and goats. They had to be rudimentary because Joan and her colleagues had only been here for a few days.

She found a girl, fourteen or fifteen years old, sitting on a large flat stone feeding the chickens seeds from a basket. "We let them run about finding insects and grubs. They're very domesticated. So far, none has left on a forest adventure." She pointed at the mouth of another cave. "At night, we put them behind a metre high stone wall. I'm sure they could escape if they wanted to, but none has."

"And in the day, you search for the hidden places where they've laid their eggs."

"Yeah. I arrive with a basket of grain, and return with a basket of eggs. Don't suppose they think it's a very good trade."

Emily glanced around, looking for the goats Joan mentioned. "What about your goats?"

"My three nannies and a billy. They're more adventuresome, but they come back at night to provide us with milk for our youngest."

The next day, after a long trek to and from Noah's hut, Emily slumped by the fire outside the main cave. Don arrived with bowls of stew and two flatbreads. "Are old man Noah's sheep as spooked as his sons say they are?"

"They seemed agitated, but otherwise healthy enough."

"Is now the time to start assembling the pieces?"

Emily stared at her flatbread. "Did someone bring the flour for baking these?"

Don nodded. "Someone did. Somehow, most of us got an inkling that the chaos was imminent. We grabbed a few things before beginning the treks that led us here. Getting back to my question, can we start?"

"What, start trying to understand what's happened in the outside world, or what's happening now on Neuvo Britannia?"

"The latter. But we should start with the first suggestion something strange was happening."

Emily said nothing for several minutes, focusing on the food Don brought her. "It starts for me a year, no, eighteen months ago when Ethan brought the dubious email about corals and his story about a talking shapeshifting bear to my attention. We investigated the email and confirmed it was a fake, and I never believed in his bear, but that was the start."

"Eighteen months fits with the start of the series of Etan's articles— outstanding pieces that were published worldwide."

"Yeah, they really were great, better than articles he'd previously published in the university newspaper. Looks like we should give some of the credit to the bear's insights, but, as I said, I didn't believe it was real."

"What changed your mind?"

"Nothing until I saw the glow on the northern horizon."

Don placed his empty bowl on the ground. "Okay, my turn. I knew nothing about Ethan's bear, so I took his articles at face value. I have no explanation for why I, along with all the others here in this refuge, independently decided last weekend it was time to run. And we all ran, many in cars, but they conked out, reducing us to walking. We ended up here and stuff we abandoned in our cars was here waiting for us. That's what we should investigate."

"Maybe thousands decided they had to seek refuge. They could have gone in many directions. The explosions and the fires would have consumed some, but others may have survived."

"True, but it doesn't change the questions. What triggered our collective decision to run? We must also explain how we covered up to a thousand kilometres, mostly on foot, burdened down with too much baggage and little children."

Emily paused again as she watched the activity around the communal fire. "Do you keep this fire burning constantly?"

Don nodded. "It keeps us and our livestock safe from predators, and we don't have an endless supply of matches."

"So where do you get the firewood? From this forest we're in?"

"Fallen branches from trees in the surrounding forest. We've also been outside in the burnt-out wastelands scrounging tree limbs that weren't entirely consumed by the fires. We decided right away we wouldn't chop down living trees in our refuge."

"That introduces several additional questions. How did this rather extensive piece of forest survive? How did possessions you abandoned with your cars get here? What made you decide to go farther afield rather than chop down nearby trees?"

"Add Ethan's bear and spooked sheep. We must conclude some unknown force is influencing our thinking. Can we discover what it is?"

9 Life in the Hidden Forest

Ethan Johnson's first year in the hidden forest was interesting, to put it mildly. He'd adjusted to his temporary life as a gnome. At least, he hoped it would be temporary. He was half as tall as he used to be and twice as round, but he'd shed his concerns for his lack of height. The fairies and many gnomes were shorter than him, and only a few elves towered over him. The other gnomes called him Coggle because he'd showed them several ways they could improve the house-building process, and he'd recently become friendly with the radiantly positive Bittybeam, a female gnome who appeared to be single and about his age.

He'd constructed, with the help of several other gnomes, a half-buried house built into the side of a hill. Its most interesting external feature was an elaborate oval door flanked by two round windows. The main floor contained the kitchen and a large room that served as dining and living rooms. The second floor, set back from the first, contained a bedroom, a bathroom, and another room. His compatriots said the extra room was for the bairns he'd soon have. When they were building Coggle's house, he thought it was too small.

Bittybeam, however, thought it was a perfect place for a brilliant thinker and his bride to raise the two offspring gnomish couples produced. Coggle sighed. *If the enchanting Bittybeam thinks my house is adequate for a family of four, I shouldn't complain.*

He was puffing his pipe and wondering about Bittybeam's intentions when an emissary from Melian, the elfin leader, arrived at his door. The pipe was a gnomish habit he'd acquired without giving it a second thought.

"Melian requests your presence at a meeting to discuss the problems in the outside world."

"Right now?" Coggle asked. They'd never invited him to Melian's palace. He expected a more formal invitation and time to prepare.

The emissary, a fairy, nodded, then asked. "You know how to find the council chamber?" He nodded, and she rose into the air.

As Coggle stood in his doorway checking the positioning of his conical red hat before pulling on his boots, she said, "quickly. I have others to inform." Without waiting for his reply, she flew off.

When he got there, Coggle realized the council chamber was not in an imperial palace. It was on the ground in a civic structure, like a town's courthouse and made almost entirely from bamboo. He learned after a few discrete inquiries that elves, including Melian, constructed their 'houses' above ground in banyan trees. They weren't houses in the normal sense, but separate rooms, all quite small with bamboo structures that supported walls and a roof made of large interwoven fronds. They had floors of bamboo canes split lengthwise. The highly agile elves flitted between rooms along tree branches. They gained access to their treetop houses through the hollow central cores of the banyan trees or with ladders made from vines they deployed from above.

Fairies didn't have houses. They simply found comfortable places among the tree limbs and smaller branches when they wanted to sleep, eat, or relax, talking to their friends.

Inside the council chamber, Coggle saw Melian, three other elves, one fairy, and twenty gnomes. One was Bittybeam.

Melian brought the meeting to order by reminding the twenty-one gnomes they promised to help the elves understand the unprecedented chaos Apexian society inflicted on their planet. She turned to a white-haired gnome who was the oldest in the room.

He cleared his throat and began in a gravelly voice. "I was an early contributor to the Society of Atomic Scientists and the Doomsday Clock, the device we used to warn everyone of the dangers of nuclear warfare. Midnight would signify the end of civilization. Since I retired from my position as physics professor, threats from the potential for nuclear war and climate change have pushed the clock to its closest approach to zero. In 2023, it was ninety seconds before midnight. Since then, it has fluctuated between ninety and sixty seconds. Our job must be to determine what pushed it from a handful of seconds before midnight to midnight."

"Thank you, Bristlebrink. We've learned several important things over the past year. We have hundreds of elfin refuges. They're all safe, spread around the globe, and all reporting similar results." Melian turned to the lone fairy in the chamber. "Aurora, what can you say about our island?"

Aurora hovered in the middle of the chamber. "Everywhere but the hidden forest and the refuge you created for animals, we see complete destruction. All buildings destroyed. All forests burned. Apexians and other animals who remain in the cities died as we watched from afar. No sign of new life. Rural areas far from the cities are more promising. Small plants are sprouting, and small animals like mice, rats, and rabbits have survived. We've only seen a few Apexian. Our scouts say there's something poisonous in the air. They cannot stay outside our forest for long."

"Thank you, Aurora," Melian said. "That's the message we're hearing around the globe." She spread her arms wide. "We turn to you, with your knowledge of Apexians and your former world, to help us make sense of it."

Melian held up her arms, palms forward, while many of the newly minted gnomes spoke over each other, trying to get their ideas heard. She waited while the other elves ushered the gnomes to the door. "Meet together, give it your most serious consideration, and return with your best answer."

They met the same afternoon in the circle of large meeting stones outside the latest cluster of gnomish houses. The males sat smoking their pipes, and the females disappeared into their homes. They returned a few minutes later with pots of tea and plates of cakes. Bittybeam had tea and cakes for Coggle. After they'd distributed the tea and cakes, and everyone had taken their seats, Bristlebrink stood, leaning on his cane. "What do we make of Melian's observations?"

Another scholarly looking gnome with slouched shoulders and rumpled appearance, but much younger than Bristlebrink, offered his opinion. "Many regional conflicts that escalated into nuclear wars."

"At the same time?" Bristlebrink asked.

The younger gnome didn't back down. "Seems unlikely, but it's the only explanation."

"I agree," Bristlebrink replied. "Simultaneous conflicts fit the observations, but we must be careful. There could be other explanations." He gazed from one face to another. "Observations from anyone else?"

"Until the day I arrived here, I'd been studying climate change," Coggle said. "We knew wildfires caused by climate change were getting worse in the last few months. They suggest a major uptick in global warming before the chaos enveloped us. How does that fit into your analysis?"

Bittybeam stood and surveyed the faces around the circle. "My focus was on political science, and the way aggressor nations were getting bolder. Many had nuclear arsenals."

"And thermobaric weapons," the middle-aged scholar added. "They could combine with Coggle's wildfires to generate truly massive conflagrations."

Several others expressed their opinions. The discussion went around in circles, focusing on the ideas raised by the middle-aged gnome whose name Coggle now knew was Bristlebud, Coggle, and Bittybeam. When the sun disappeared over the horizon, the meeting broke up. Everyone returned to their individual homes to prepare their evening meals.

His simple meal complete, Coggle sat in his gnome-sized armchair, gazing at the magical elfin forest. His thoughts were on Bittybeam, not the critical problem Melian tasked them with solving. He now knew Bittybeam was, like him, an alpha transformed into a gnome. When he became a gnome, they told him he was now 135 years old—equivalent to his prior age of twenty-seven. *Would that make Bittybeam about 120?*

He'd assumed, since early in his days as a gnome, that all the alphas in this forest came from a relatively small area of their natural lands. He had no proof, but Melian said elves, fairies, and gnomes from several elfin forests accepted animals and specially chosen refugees. It seemed logical they came from distinct areas. Was Bittybeam a political science student from South Serene University? It was the only one on their island. Were other students or faculty from their university living amongst them?

A thumping noise from outside his little house distracted him. He couldn't see anything because the window was rather high on his front wall, but someone, or something, was outside, banging on that wall near ground level. He pulled on his boots, grabbed the stout walking stick he used for his frequent hikes, and investigated.

Outside, he found a rather slender female gnome. At least, he assumed she was female because she wore a bright green hat, like all females, from infancy until they were married. She also had the long blond braids that characterized growing girls. Had someone tangled her in a cocoon of vines with sharp thorns from her neck to her ankles and left her lying on the ground, kicking his wall?

Coggle helped her turn so her back was against his wall and began unravelling the vines. "How did this happen?" he asked.

"Lifablink and Sneeb. I hate them," she replied as she tried to squirm, but only dug the thorns deeper into her skin. "They caught me here watching your house and said they'd teach me a lesson."

"I see. And why were you watching my house?"

"Bittybeam, our mistress, likes you, and I wanted to learn why?"

"Bittybeam. What's she mistress of?"

"The orphan house. I like her. She's kind, but Lifablink and Sneeb are mean. Then there's Mopple. He's harmless, always playing with clocks."

"And your name is?"

"Fidgow. I sometimes have good ideas, but I lack confidence."

Coggle pulled away the last piece of bramble. "Five of you living in the orphan house." He looked at the darkening sky. "I think you should lead the way, and we'll explain everything to Bittybeam."

"I can't do that. Lifablink and Sneeb will make my life worse than ever."

"I fear you must. You and Bittybeam will sort out something. Maybe you'll have one of your good ideas."

10 A little Romance

"No! Never! I can't go back there," Fidgow said, as Coggle half-dragged her along the path to the orphan house. It was truly dark when they arrived.

Bittybeam met them on the threshold. "I understand what Lifablink and Sneeb did. I've sent them to bed without supper. They won't bother you again."

"But they will. As soon as the lights are out, it will start all over again."

"You need to stand up to them. You're older, and smarter. Don't let them get to you," Bittybeam said. "Come inside, get some supper, and you, Coggle, and I will sort everything out."

Bittybeam surprised Coggle by including him in the deliberations. He'd hoped he'd be free after he brought Fidgow home, relatively unharmed, but he said nothing. He was becoming infatuated with Bittybeam. It now looked like she shared at least some of his interest.

Coggle and Bittybeam drank tea while Fidgow consumed a prodigious quantity of the stew Bittybeam had prepared for her charges' dinner. When she finished eating, the three of them discussed their options. After a discussion that solved nothing, Fidgow crept upstairs to fetch her bedroll and night things.

She returned seconds later and placed her finger to her lips. Coggle and Bittybeam followed her upstairs, and she pointed at the bucket propped on the top of the door to the girls' bedroom. Coggle steadied the bucket as Bittybeam flung open the door.

"Is this your idea of a joke?" she asked. Her voice was tense, but surprisingly quiet, little more than a whisper. She gestured for the bucket, then turned to the two miscreants who were clinging to each other. She pointed at their bedrolls. When they sat down, still clinging to each other, Bittybeam dumped the contents of the bucket over their heads.

The girls screeched, but Bittybeam showed no mercy. "Deal with it!" she said, as she stomped from the room, followed by Coggle and Fidgow. Fidgow slammed the door behind her, but didn't giggle or smirk.

When they returned to the main floor, Coggle made his excuses and prepared to leave, but Bittybeam forestalled him. "Let me get Fidgow settled. Then we can have more tea outside, where we can have a private conversation. It's a pleasant evening, and I can't take my idea for solving Fidgow's problem to the matron for all orphans without first discussing it with you."

Outside, Goggle, who felt like he was swimming in tea, stared at her three sitting stones, a larger one on the left and two smaller ones facing it. He chose the larger one; hoping Bittybeam would join him there. About ten minutes later, Bittybeam joined him on the larger stone. She had a teacup in each hand.

She began without preamble. "Poor girl. She is just far too shy. I know why. Her parents mistreated her before she landed in our care."

"I didn't think the mistreatment of children happened in this magical land," Coggle replied.

"Uncommon, but not unknown. But that's not our problem. Our problem is what we do now." She paused as she sipped her tea. "Something she said after she finished her dinner got me thinking."

Coggle worried that any solution involving his input would be a serious incursion into his trouble-free existence, thinking about his fate while solving a few technical problems for his fellow gnomes. He saw no benefit in postponing the inevitable. "Yes," he said to encourage her.

"If she moved into your house as your housekeeper, it would further her education and help prepare her for the day she gets married with a house of her own to manage." She held up her hand when Coggle opened his mouth. "And one more thing. If she was relaxed and happier, it might be all she needs to…" She paused as her cheeks reddened. "Well, you know what I'm talking about. She's too old for the day she becomes a young woman."

"You want me to take part in that? Seems totally inappropriate!"

Bittybeam put down her cup and took Coggles free hand. "I want you to provide a peaceful, caring environment. Somewhere she can relax, thinking someone appreciates her efforts. I'll provide the womanly advice if our idea is successful."

Coggle wandered home, thinking about the scheme Bittybeam concocted after talking to Fidgow. She was following up on one of Fidgow's ideas, and it now included him as a co-conspirator. He hoped it was one of her good ideas, but it seemed like a plan fraught with difficulty, one that could easily blow up in their faces. What was he to do? If he refused to take part, Bittybeam could end their friendship. That was too much to bear. When he arrived home, he began cleaning the smaller of his two bedrooms.

Bittybeam bounded up to Coggle's house the next afternoon. He was outside, clearing away the thorny vines he'd left strewn about when he freed her young charge.

"It's all set," she said while gazing at his well-maintained house. "Only one tiny problem. Your betrothal to a suitable adult gnome is required before she moves in here."

He stood with his mouth hanging open as he tried to process this latest development.

She pressed her point. "We may be stuck here for years, living as gnomes among the elves, fairies, and real gnomes. Gnomes like us, transformed by magic, mustn't marry the real gnomes. We've been close for ages and ideally suited. You don't want to miss romantic relationships during your young vigorous years, do you?"

He shook his head. "Some romance would go down nicely during those long winter evenings, but we've hardly known each other for ages."

She huffed, but Coggle knew it was only for effect. "Speak for yourself. I've been aware of you since our first weeks in this magical world. I've noticed all the useful things you do so willingly for others, and the way Bristlebrink listened carefully to your ideas and engaged in serious discussions about them."

"He listened just as seriously to your ideas."

"Quit trying to change my focus. We're perfectly suited. We have very few options in the forest, and probably even fewer outside it. Why shouldn't we enjoy our betrothal and its benefits?"

"But not the joys of raising children."

"Not until we get married. But then the idea of two tykes livening up those long winter evenings seems quite appealing."

"Two? Wouldn't it be better to start with one and see how it goes?"

She kissed him. "I'm glad you agree, but you must realize gnomish couplings invariably produce twins."

11 The Big Problem

By the end of his second year in the elfin forest community, Coggle felt comfortable in its gnomish society. He'd found his niche as an ideas man, or is that, ideas gnome. It wasn't difficult because gnomes were rather stubborn, sticking to their old solutions even when they stopped working. Coggle would suggest fresh approaches. The gnomes would try them and go away happy when they worked. That's how he got his name, Coggle, the idea generator.

It was quite simple, with no magic required. He considered how he'd have solved the problems before the chaos brought him into the hidden forest and applied his old understanding.

Coggle found the communalistic economic system harder to accept. Everyone—gnomes, fairies, and elves—contributed what they could and claimed what they needed for their simple lifestyles. Their system worked, but it appeared so subject to abuse. *Did low-level magic keep everyone honest, or was it something in the water supply?*

Fidgow, his new 'housekeeper', was a case in point. When she started working for him, she perused his pantry, making a list. She said she knew what provisions they needed, and where she could get them. She disappeared with her basket and returned with it overflowing. Fidgow even topped up his supply of pipe tobacco. How did the merchants know she was now getting provisions for herself and her male master, rather than the four children and one adult female living in the orphan house?

She was hard-working and happy. Every day she gained confidence, and her culinary efforts, adequate from the first days, were getting more adventuresome and reliable. No question. She made Coggle's life easier.

One day, about four months after she joined Coggle's household, she came to him after breakfast, with her eyes lowered and her posture stooped. "I need to visit Bittybeam. Is it okay if I go now?"

Coggle nodded, and she scurried out without another word. She and Bittybeam arrived about two hours later. Fidgow went straight to the kitchen to prepare lunch.

Bittybeam pulled a chair close to Coggle's. She was always smiling, but this time her cheshire cat grin looked like it could dislocate her jaw. "Told

43

you, didn't I. All she needed was somewhere away from the orphan house where she could relax."

When Coggle stared slack-jawed, she continued. "You can't pretend you didn't notice the changes." Coggle shook his head. "Well, you should have. Fidgow has become a young woman without you noticing."

Coggle smiled. "But I'm betrothed to the most intoxicating woman. I never look at anyone else."

"Well, that makes me happy, but you must notice the new dress she's making for herself. It's bigger, you know, up here." She plumped her rather noticeable breasts, "make sure you say something complimentary, because she's rather shy about the changes."

Weeks later, Bittybeam and Coggle returned to the orphan house after another stressful meeting of the gnomes tasked with understanding the human motivation that produced the two-year-old chaos.

Two toddler-sized gnome children pounced on Coggle as he settled into the oversized, at least for gnomes, armchair. Bittybeam called it their cuddling chair and the two newcomers had that purpose figured out.

"Rompus and Tifamyn," Bittybeam said before Coggle could ask. "Someone left them on our doorstep. No idea where they came from."

Sneeb struggled in with a large tray. She placed it on a table near Coggle's chair and turned to Bittybeam. "Lifablink's at the market and Mopple's in his room as usual. If you'll look after these ruffians, I'd like to meet my friend."

"What caused our meetings to become so shambolic?" Bittybeam asked, after Sneeb skipped down the steps.

"She seems happier," Coggle said as he bounced the two youngsters on his knees, "and Lifablink's taking on more responsibility. Looks like all's well in the orphan house."

Bittybeam nodded, as Tifamyn slithered to the floor and gathered a biscuit for Coggle. "All's well here, and Fidgow's a major success, but you're ignoring my question."

Coggle sighed as he broke off pieces of biscuit, one for Tifamyn and the other for Rompus, and popped the rest in his mouth before helping Tifamyn onto the cuddling chair. "The problem is Bristlebrink's fading health, and Bristlebud's changing attitude. He's become an aggressive opponent of everyone's ideas."

"Why would he do that?"

"He expects a diminishing role for Bristlebrink, and the need for a new leader. He wants that job."

"That makes no sense. He's annoying everyone. He'll have no allies if it comes to a change in leadership."

"Not if Bristlebud plans to approach Melian, saying the group needs a dynamic leader, and he's the only one who can fill that role."

"Crap, oops, sorry for the swearword," replied Bittybeam. "He's no dynamic leader. He's destroying the progress we're making."

Lifablink, carrying a large basket of produce, and Fidgow, weighed down by Coggle's stew pot, arrived linked at the elbow. Tifamyn and Rompus slid off Coggle's chair, looking for treats in Lifablink's basket. The ensuing kerfuffle drew Mopple from his room. He settled beside Coggle with questions about a clockwork mechanism he was constructing.

After the dust settled, Lifablink and Fidgow disappeared into Bittybeam's kitchen to prepare an evening feast for eight, and Mopple to his room to incorporate Coggle's suggestions into his project.

Bittybeam returned to the problems with their dysfunctional committee. "What can we do about Bristlebud?"

"Cut him off at the pass," Coggle said. "We can produce a document that synthesizes the views of the other members, give it to Bristlebrink, and ask him to present it to Melian."

"But would he? Bristlebud's his protégé."

"He was at first, but that's changed. We'll find he feels responsible for the way Bristlebud's destroying our work. He'll welcome the opportunity to set things straight."

"You think we should prepare this document, consulting the others privately about how we incorporate their ideas? When it's the best we can make it, we give it to Bristlebrink?"

"Exactly. We give Bristlebrink the opportunity for final edits and revisions and ask him to present it to Melian."

Bittybeam rose and wandered to the kitchen door. "Where are Tifamyn and Rompus?" she asked Lifablink. Lifablink pointed to a corner where the two youngest members of the orphan house family were playing with some cooking pots. Bittybeam returned to her living room. "We must keep Bristlebud in the dark and generate a killer document. Like acing the report for a major term project. Can we do it?"

Coggle put his arms around her shoulders. "We can do it. In fact, we must do it, and we must start right away."

12 A Confrontation

With his pipe clenched between his jaws and smoke curling toward the ceiling, Coggle threw himself into his new commitment to the elfin forest. His task was intellectually challenging and potentially critical to the forest's future. It came with another benefit. He and Bittybeam would tackle it together.

He had fewer commitments, so he handled most of the work. But Bittybeam wasn't a passive partner. She wrote an extensive section on the aggressive tendencies of many, mostly autocratic regimes, and the increasing unwillingness of more progressive countries to intervene when the aggressors expanded their borders at the expense of smaller, less powerful neighbours.

Bittybeam also led the consultations with the other gnomish visitors. She could easily visit their colleagues without drawing attention to her true purpose. They knew Bristlebud was keeping tabs on Coggle's movements, but it would never occur to him to follow Bittybeam. *He was such a misogynist!*

Coggle's job was to put all the disparate elements together in a comprehensive document. When they finally took their treatise to Bristlebrink, he sat reading silently for many minutes, offering no comments or making any marks in their text.

"Excellent," he said when he finished reading. "You've presented a superb synopsis of what should have been our committee's findings." Bristlebrink paused, gazing anxiously around his house. "My wonderful wife of sixty years is standing guard outside. She'll tell Bristlebud I'm sleeping if he approaches. A plausible explanation, because it's what I do most days."

"Bristlebud," Bittybeam said after Bristlebrink recovered from his moment of uncertainty. "Several fairies have kept him at a distance when we consulted our colleagues. What do you think is behind his obstructionist behaviour?"

"Bringing him here with Mildred and me was the biggest mistake I ever made. I thought he wanted to continue my work, but I was wrong. He has an unknown agenda. One I don't trust. But please, let's not dwell on an old gnome's failings." He held up the pages containing the results of Coggle and Bittybeam's labours. "How can I help with this initiative?"

"Take it to Melian and present it to her as the product of our committee's—"

"Excluding Bristlebud," Bittybeam added, before Coggle could finish his sentence.

"Oh dear," Bristlebrink replied. "I fear I'm incapable of as short a trip as one to the council chamber."

"Then we'll ask Melian to meet you here."

"Will she come? Will it be safe?"

"She will. She brought us here and will be eager to see the results of our labours. The fairies will protect her."

Bristlebrink sighed before turning to Coggle. "I keep forgetting about the fairies and the importance of their magic. I task you with contacting Melian and telling her I have several important messages to convey before I die. Now, please, I'm tired. Let me rest in peace."

Two days later, Fidgow scurried into Coggle's sitting room. "There's a fairy hovering near the door. She must have a message for you."

Coggle strode to his front door and glanced out, expecting to see Aurora. He'd contacted her right after the meeting with Bristlebrink and was hoping for a reply. The message the new fairy delivered showed him events had developed more quickly than he expected.

"Melian requests your presence at a meeting at Bristlebrink's house," she said.

Fidgow stood spellbound, gazing childlike from behind Coggle. "Would you like a cup of tea?" she asked.

"Thank you," the fairy replied, "but not just yet. I have one more errand. I'll return for tea."

Fidgow fidgeted, shifting from foot to foot as Coggle put on his boots. "Is it okay? May I invite a fairy to tea? Should I take the tea outside or will she come inside?"

Coggle smiled. She'd already made the invitation. "Inside, I suspect, but let her choose. And no cakes. She'll want nothing but tea."

Coggle sprinted toward Bristlebrink's, knowing he'd pass the orphan house along the way. He couldn't maintain the flying speed of a fairy, but if he hurried, he might catch them before Bittybeam departed. He stopped after too much unaccustomed running fifty metres from the orphan house and leaned over with his hands on his knees, breathing hard. A minute later, they emerged from her house, Bittybeam turning toward

Bristlebrink's and the fairy back the way she came. She swooped low when she reached Coggle and gave him a friendly wave.

He wondered as he rushed to catch Bittybeam, if the fairy orchestrated her tea date with Fidgow, and if so, why?

Inside Bristlebrink's house, he, Mildred, and Melian were sitting around a low table drinking the obligatory cups of tea. Mildred poured tea for Coggle and Bittybeam, and Melian addressed Bristlebrink. "Coggle says you have a document for me."

Bristlebrink cleared his throat. "More Coggle and Bittybeam's work than mine, but it's the document we should have produced weeks ago if Bristlebud hadn't constantly disrupted our discussions."

"We'll worry about Bristlebud later," Melian replied. "First, I'd like you to present your findings."

Bristlebrink glanced at Coggle and Bittybeam, who nodded, before placing his copy of their assessment on the table. "Our story is quite simple, and consistent with our knowledge of how Apexian societies worked, and the information gathered by elfin communities around the world in the days before chaos engulfed the planet."

Melian held up her right hand. "Temperate to subpolar regions with extensive forests. Those are our domain. We have few observations for other regions."

Bristlebrink nodded his old white-haired head. "We acknowledge the limitations imposed by your areas with observational data and have adjusted our conclusions accordingly. We must start 150 years ago at the end of the Second Great War. I'll let Bittybeam explain how developments a century and a half ago set the stage for the events of two years ago."

"The period that followed the Second Great War was a standoff between mostly autocratic powers with territorial ambitions and more progressive democratic powers that wanted to rely on global institutions and their willingness to act when necessary to keep world peace. It worked reasonably well for sixty-five years."

"Then what happened?" Bristlebrink asked when Bittybeam paused for a breath. He must have known the answer, so he was, in his professorial way, asking her to continue.

"The progressive powers lost their will to intervene, to threaten to use overwhelming military power to keep the aggressors from rolling over weaker nations. It wasn't an abrupt change, but a gradual one that gave the aggressor nations the upper hand in recent decades." Bittybeam paused, looking toward Bristlebrink for guidance. He made circles with his forefinger and she carried on.

"That brings us to five years ago and the three countries that could have orchestrated the calamity that engulfed us. They are Cathay, Novorussia, and the North Columbian Union. The next observations are Coggles."

"Yes," Coggle replied as he shuffled his pages. "For the second half of the period Bittybeam's described, greenhouse gas emissions held steady. Higher than they should be, but they've been stable. It all changed four years ago. Levels started increasing for no discernable reason, and by the time the chaos unfolded, they were increasing rapidly."

"Did anyone know why?" Melian asked.

Coggle shook his head. "Outside observers couldn't understand it, but the perpetrators obviously knew. It had to be one of the three largest nuclear powers. The only logical candidate is Novorussia."

Melian raised her arm. "Why them? Why not another major producer of green-house-gas-generating fuels?"

"Because the only sensible answer was a large autocratic country with extensive mostly unpopulated forests that was a major producer and consumer of fossil fuels and a nuclear power."

"Ah," she replied. "I get it. Novorussia concluded the other nuclear powers would tolerate tactical nuclear weapons, but to be sure, they orchestrated a resurgence of forest fires to distract everyone when they deployed them."

At that point, Bristlebud burst through Bristlebrink's front door. Six fairies flew in behind him.

"Give me those reports. They're fabrications, not based on any concrete evidence, and unauthorized by me."

"We'll do nothing of the sort," Melian replied. "If you try to harm anyone or take the documents by force, we'll restrain you."

"That old fart," Bristlebud said, pointing at Bristlebrink, "I should put him out of his misery. The others should return to what they were doing before you established your foolish committee."

He took one step toward Bristlebrink and fell to the ground, writhing in pain.

13 Romance and New Responsibilities

Coggle slumped into his chair. When Bristlebud threatened violence, Coggle rose to challenge him. Bristlebud was a typical bully, all bluster and threat, but during a confrontation, he'd lack courage. Coggle wouldn't find out if his assessment was correct. Elfin or fairy magic stole his opportunity to subdue Bristlebud and impress Bittybeam with his fighting prowess. Probably for the best. He suspected Bittybeam would prefer a diplomat who diffused a situation with words to someone who relied on fisticuffs.

Melian placed her hand on his arm. "I'm confident you would've handled him, but this is tidier, with less broken furniture. The fairies will take Bristlebud to the council chamber, and I'll deal with him." She turned to Bristlebrink. "If you're not too tired—"

"Tired!" Bristlebrink replied. "Most excitement I've seen in ages. Mildred was ready with her frypan. We could've helped Coggle subdue that young fool. Made me feel young again."

Melian laughed, a polite little chuckle. "Well, I'm glad that wasn't necessary. I'd like to continue our conversation for a few minutes if you're up to it."

Bristlebrink nodded as Mildred held their door for the six fairies. They had Bristlebud restrained in a web of fine twine. Outside, four grabbed corners, and flew away with Bristlebud beneath them, trapped like a fly in a spider's web. The others stayed behind to guard their leader.

Melian glanced from Bittybeam, Coggle, and Bristlebrink, sitting around his table, to Mildred listening from her kitchen doorway. "I'll share your findings with leaders of the other hidden forests. If you have any other ideas, please bring them to me, but we can now consider your project complete. I hope everyone involved, but especially Coggle, is ready for another adventure." She paused, eyebrows raised as if she expected questions. When no one piped up, she continued. "We must now look forward to the future of our island realm."

"The northern third," Coggle said, "is mostly flatlands. Outside of Kingstown, our capital and only proper city, it's cultivated, or at least it was, with very few natural spaces. To the southeast of Kingstown was Eastport, our only commercial and military harbour, and west of Eastport, the island's commercial and military airport. If you drew a line east to west across the island starting about twenty kilometres south of Eastport, the remaining terrain becomes hilly. It was almost entirely forested."

Bittybeam scowled. "The university is in the forest near your east-west line."

"Along with two small villages," Coggle added. "A small fishing village on the coast and a larger inland one nearer the university. Put the three together and you have the community known as University. There are other fishing villages along the east coast, and various hamlets within the forest."

Bittybeam turned to Melian. "Where is this taking us? Someone bombed Kingstown, Eastport, and the airport into oblivion, and the fires destroyed everything else. Can anyone be alive?"

"We sent out scouting parties, brief forays protected as best we can with our magic. They've detected Apexian life in a resort south of Kingstown and at the university. Scattered survivors in the forest."

"But how did they survive?"

"Subbasements in urban buildings and some of the larger university buildings. Elsewhere in the forested regions, natural cave systems could have protected them from the initial blasts," Coggle suggested. "My question would be how they found food?"

"Good questions," Melian replied, taking back the initiative. "Ones we hope to answer. To accomplish this, we need an emissary. I'm suggesting Coggle could fill that role." She paused, giving her four listeners a chance to digest what she'd said. "It's getting late, and I can see Bristlebrink is tiring. Rambleroot will lead these missions supported by teams of fairies. We'll make them as safe as possible."

Later, after he bid Bittybeam adieu outside the orphan house, Coggle had much to consider. First, he could abandon any lingering thoughts he wasn't pulling his weight in the elfin forest. Second, he didn't know how he, an Apexian transformed into a gnome, could be a useful emissary. Did Melian think he could convince suspicious alphas he was one of them? It may be a lot easier for a magic-wielding elf or fairy to convince someone struggling to survive that they could be useful allies. He hadn't resolved these issues when he arrived home to what might develop into another problem.

Fidgow greeted him inside his door. "Dela's visit was so good. She stayed for so long and had two cups of tea and a small piece of cake. I had my cake and most of hers, but she was so nice and interested in everything I do. She told me something that's really important."

51

"Oh," said Coggle, "what's that?"

"Rambleroot likes me. He works with Dela and always talks about me."

Coggle shook his head. *This being a pseudo-parent was becoming complicated.* "How do you know Rambleroot?"

"I met him at the market when he was collecting provisions for his aging parents. Now I see him, sometimes only briefly, on many of my trips to the market."

"You know what else he does?"

"He's a scout. He learns about conditions outside our forest."

"That's dangerous work. He might not return from one of those expeditions."

Fidgow nodded, her eyes wide and sparkly. "We've talked about it. Isn't it romantic?"

Coggle had no answer to such a question. He strode to his favourite chair for a long think. He filled and lit his pipe before turning his thoughts to the big question. How could he, in his current gnomish form, approach alphas and generate the understanding and rapport Melian needed?

He woke up several hours later. His pipe was safe in its ashtray—Fidgow must have rescued it and prevented it from starting a fire. The answer to his question was obvious. He would transform from gnome to Apexian, just like the bear he'd encountered in his apartment had transformed into a wolf, then a deer, and finally, a tiger.

The only question was how he'd gain the magic he needed for the transformation.

14 Developments in the Animal Refuge

After two years, living in what appeared to be the only surviving forest in Neuvo Britannica, Emily Dickson's view of her world had shifted. Nothing had contradicted the conclusions she and Don Grant came to about external forces. One or more nuclear bombs detonated over Kingstown and Eastport. Wildfires enhanced by the hottest and driest conditions Neuvo Britannica had ever seen rampaged at record speed across the entire island. Thermobaric bombs exploding over the northern third of their island probably added to the conflagration. Electromagnetic pulses destroyed electronic communications and disabled the vehicles many of the refugees used to escape the northern sector. Impossible to confirm, but no other conclusions fit their initial observations.

Their other observations were more nebulous and more disconcerting. They led to conclusions modern alphas would never accept, but the inexplicable observations kept increasing. For Emily, three observations stood out.

The first was how she survived the rampaging wildfires. They were too hot and the light blinding. The air became suffocating in the hours it took for the fire to pass over the pond where she sheltered. The compresses on her eyes when she finally awoke were made of an unknown fabric and smelled of an unknown but obviously highly effective medicine. No way she could've walked from that pond to this forest, but here she was hale and hearty with no lingering effects of her ordeal.

Second, she was the first to decide the only solution to increased crowding in the communal cave—their group had grown by seven adults and three more children—was houses built on the flatter land a few hundred metres east of their mountain cave. She built, with a little help from Don, a tiny bamboo house. Emily knew precious little about house construction, and even less about bamboo as the construction material. Don was no more knowledgeable, but the house went up surprisingly easily. Several times, when she reached trickier spots in the construction process, she wasn't happy with her efforts. But when she returned to her building task on the next day, someone with expertise had redone the questionable bit of construction. Neither Don, nor any of the others, admitted to doing the repairs, and they always occurred in the dead of night. *Was a bashful secret admirer unwilling to claim credit?* She thought not. There were just no suitable candidates in their tiny population.

Her other observation was harder to explain. On five occasions, she needed medications to relieve problems with the community's goats and Noah's sheep. She had no medications or knowledge of herbal remedies she might substitute, but on each occasion, herbal remedies appeared. They all worked, more slowly, but ultimately as effectively as the modern medicines. Joan insisted none of the thirty-two adults were herbalists. *Who produced the herbal remedies?* Her hypothetical secret admirer was not a viable explanation because she'd described the veterinary problems to no one.

One day, when Emily was off ministering to Noah's sheep, Marc Lebrun arrived with stories of creepy magical creatures. He was spouting off about the need to eliminate them before creating a libertarian state in Neuvo Britannia when Joan Jessop asked him how he could contribute to their community. He stood and puffed out his chest. "I will lead you in the quest for a libertarian state that will rule the world. In step one, we'll rid Neuvo Britannica of the vermin that held me captive for the last two years. Next, we'll eliminate any alphas who refuse to join our epic quest. Then, with Neuvo Britannica as a base, we'll free the world from all malignant forces. We'll produce a worldwide libertarian utopia."

Joan ignored his rant. "But how will you contribute to our little community in the next days and weeks?"

"What! I will do what I just said—lead this group to glory." He turned to the alphas who'd gathered. "Are you with me?"

When no one responded, something Joan expected because she was a low-keyed but well-liked leader, she buried the knife. "What should it be, up on his croft, helping old Noah with his sheep? Rory would like the opportunity to move on."

Marc turned and stomped down the path, past the growing numbers of bamboo houses to the forest.

"I hope the grumpy old bear," someone said, "the one who frightens the children when they stomp off to avoid doing their chores, is lurking. That fool will be back after dumping a load in his pants."

When Emily returned from Noah's croft, she found a group that was far more agitated than usual. She sought Don Grant, knowing he'd have a level-headed explanation for whatever was bothering everyone.

"A new refugee, someone named Marc Lebrun," Don said. "He's sure full of himself. Spouting libertarianism ideas of our glorious future when his adherents wipe out any opponents, including magical creatures who'd kept him captive for the past two years. He called it a utopian future, but it sounded like a fascist dystopia to me."

"Marc Lebrun! I knew him, a student in our invasive species research group. He came from a North Columbian oil-producing region, and he didn't fit in. Claimed he was a mathematical modeller interested in ecological problems, but it was all crap. His models were pseudoscience sponsored by the energy cartels to defend high levels of carbon emissions."

"He was in the biology department with you and Ethan Johnson when the chaos erupted?"

Emily shook her head before slumping onto one of the large flat stones surrounding the constantly lit fire outside their main cave. "Left in disgrace sometime earlier when we exposed the stupidity of his models. He landed a job with emeritus professor Abercrombie helping him produce his memoirs."

"Physics professor Abercrombie?"

"Yeah, Dr. Charles Abercrombie. He was about ninety, but still active, working on his memoirs and giving the odd lecture. Lebrun was good at spinning yarns about everything he could accomplish. He must have overwhelmed the old professor with one hell of a sales pitch. We paid little attention, just glad he was gone from our invasive species group."

After a few minutes, Emily leaned forward. "Lebrun said something about evil creatures who kept him captive. Did he describe them?"

"Said they were magical, but offered no physical description."

"Interesting." Emily rose and made four circuits of the firepit before sitting again beside Don. "What if they aren't evil? What if they're friendly or at least benign and responsible for all the things we can't explain?"

"And they saw through some scheme Lebrun was promoting and kicked him out of their domain and he landed here?"

Emily took Don's hands in hers. "Makes sense, doesn't it? And it could explain most, maybe even all, of the observations we can't explain."

"But who are they, and where do they live?"

"And why was Lebrun living amongst them?" Emily added.

15 Coggle's Adventures on the Outside

Weeks later, Coggle was outside in the real world, hiding behind some bushes and rubble from a university building. He, Rambleroot, Dela, and five other fairies were watching a young alpha checking snares she'd set to catch rabbits. She had quite a haul, three it appeared, when she reset her last snare and retreated into the remains of the teaching facilities at one end of the physics building.

Nothing happened for most of an hour while Coggle completed his temporary transition back into his Ethan Johnson persona. Then they noticed smoke and the aroma of roasting meat coming from the teaching facilities.

Rambleroot led their team to the building's opposite end. When they arrived at a point that seemed meaningful to Rambleroot, he held up his hand and called for silence. "Listen," he said, his voice only a whisper. "Don't you hear it?"

Coggle strained without success to hear any sound in the eerie silence until Dela waved them to a spot where she hovered. She pointed down, and Coggle crept forward to investigate. He located a pipe, perhaps ten centimetres in diameter. It was the obvious source of the humming noise Rambleroot's more sensitive gnomish ears picked up from several metres away.

Coggle peered at the wires protruding from the end of the pipe, but didn't touch them. He then backed away and retreated from the rubble that was once the physics building as silently as he could.

Outside, behind their barrier of rubble and bushes, he addressed Rambleroot and the fairies. "Definitely a noise I'd associate with electrical equipment. Can we wait until after dark to see if light escapes from that pipe?"

Rambleroot shook his head. "Not sure you can remain in your Apexian form for that long, and we're so far north, I'm concerned about the effects of radiation on all of us. We shouldn't remain outside our forest until tomorrow."

"But," Coggle said. "That alphan female is out catching rabbits without apparent harm."

56

"Apparent harm," Rambleroot replied. "We don't know how long she stays outside, and you said before, they must take risks to find food."

"No problem," Dela said. "Coggle can return to his gnomish form and you can head back. I'll stay here and check the pipe after dark."

Rambleroot scratched his chin. "Should work, but Iridessa should stay with you. We'll leave when Coggle completes his transformation with four fairies. If you leave as soon as you confirm there is or is not light coming from that pipe, you'll catch us before we reach the safety of the hidden forest."

"Light, quite bright and steady, not flickering like candles or a fire," Dela said when she and Iridessa caught up before dawn.

"Electricity, almost for sure," Coggle said. "Next question is, how are they generating it?"

Coggle's next assignment was more difficult. Melian wanted him to infiltrate a group of alphas in Uplands, a holiday village in the mountain foothills south southwest of Kingstown. Some lived in the basements of destroyed buildings and others in houses designed to withstand forest fires. Their rhetoric was fiery, a complex mixture of libertarian and anti-woke politics spiced with territorial ambitions. Coggle's task—figure out their agenda for a population in their island domain that couldn't exceed a few hundred Apexians.

Dela learned of a meeting of their target group, and Coggle once more transformed into his alphan form, this time for a mission where they would certainly notice him. He snuck into the back of the meeting in the subbasement of a large burned-out building, hoping to remain inconspicuous while he listened to their leader. He didn't remain anonymous for long.

"Hello stranger," a large fierce-looking character in a military uniform, complete with a pretentious peaked cap, said as he sidled up too close for comfort.

"Just arrived from South Cape," Coggle replied. "Life's tough down there. Food's in short supply, and with winter approaching…I'm reporting back on our options."

"Listen away. Our leaders should answer your questions. Just one piece of advice. No one leaves before the meeting ends."

Coggle listened, hearing nothing that suggested he or anyone else should cast their lot with this bunch of crazy fascists. He heard endless statements of their bright future, but nothing explaining how they would get there. And nothing about the territorial ambitions Melian said they harboured.

When the meeting ended, Coggle joined a group heading for the exit, but the military officer he'd encountered earlier barred his way.

"Sorry bud, but newcomers can't leave until they agree to join our mission. We'll give you tonight to think about it from one of our luxury suites, and in the morning, you can give us your decision."

Two scrawnier soldiers grabbed Coggle's arms and marched him to a room that was a minimally equipped cell. Some choice, Coggle thought as he stumbled into the cell. *If I don't agree to join them, will they force me to do so anyway? Or do they execute anyone who opposes them?* He sat on the thin mattress on his cell's single cot and pondered his fate.

What would happen now? Could he remain in Apexian form until his first opportunity to escape? Or would the magic wear off, and he'd wake up back in his gnomish form? He was considering these questions when Dela's head emerged from a duct built into the ceiling. She lowered a thick rope and encouraged him to climb.

He hadn't climbed ropes since physical education classes in high school, but he soon remembered the technique.

"Climb into the duct and crawl to the first junction," Dela said when he reached the ceiling. "I'll replace the grill and meet you there."

By the time they reached the place where Dela entered the duct, the guards had noticed Coggle's absence, and much noise accompanied an apparently disorganized search. Dela watched Coggle transform into his gnomish form for a few minutes before transforming into an Apexian mother. "This will work fine," she said as she stuffed a ball cap low over Coggle's ears and produced a basket of vegetables she passed to him. She'd hidden his conical hat at the bottom. "You're my child, and we're on our way home from the market. If we encounter any gendarmes, keep your head down."

She jumped from the duct and strode off at a fast pace. Coggle struggled to keep up. They were soon outside the village and into scrubland, where four fairies waited for them. Seconds later, Dela had resumed her fairy form. Coggle had lost his basket of veggies and his ball cap, but he had his red conical hat perched on his head. They set off at a rapid pace. Before dawn broke, they were halfway home.

When they reached the hidden forest, Melian greeted them with another problem. "As you know, we removed the magic that kept Bristlebud in his gnomish form. He reverted to an Apexian, and we left him in the larger forest we're maintaining for the animals. The Apexians living there soon tired of his stupid behaviour and they've dumped him in the wasteland outside their forest."

"Can they do that?" Coggle asked. "I thought your hidden forest and the animals' forest had impenetrable barriers."

"Here, we're protected by impenetrable mountains. The animals' forest is not, but we control movements through its boundaries. The Apexians must get out to collect firewood. On one of their trips, they left Bristlebud on the outside, and we're keeping him out."

"He's dangerous. Aren't you worried if you leave him wandering around outside? He could cause trouble."

"We're monitoring the situation," Melian said. "It's the best we can do for the moment."

16 An Alpha for Good?

Coggle fell into a routine that kept him away from Bittybeam for extended periods. Not his preferred outcome, but he couldn't forget Melian welcomed him and several dozen others into the elfin forest as their entire island burst into flames. He owed them an enormous debt.

Day after day, he ventured forth with Rambleroot, Dela, and her team of fairies to check on the health of Apexian communities in the southern half of their island home. Coggle knew these communities were often hundreds of kilometres apart, but they always reached them after less than five hours of marching through the burnt-out forests. Obviously, fairy magic sped them on their way to whatever destination Melian chose. The numbers in these communities were invariably tiny, just a handful of survivors struggling to feed themselves. None shared the aggressive ambitions of the vigilante army he'd encountered in Uplands, the holiday village southwest of Kingstown.

When they'd surveyed the last of the villages on their list, they returned to the hidden forest. Coggle expected a longer stay in what he now considered his home. It would be his opportunity to discuss with Bittybeam their future together. Fidgow and Rambleroot had been stepping out for some time, and he was sure Rambleroot had a marriage proposal on his mind. He thought he and Bittybeam should have similar romantic thoughts, but Bittybeam was strangely standoffish whenever he tried to broach the subject.

"I can't tell you how I know," she said, "but our time here may soon be over. We shouldn't be talking about the future until we know how that plays out."

One day, Melian summonsed the scouting parties and most Apexians who'd transformed into gnomes for a large meeting with her elfin council. Elves and gnomes on the main floor and fairies in perches around the perimeter filled the room when Coggle arrived. He'd fallen into a bad habit from his alphan days of arriving late at meetings. He crowded into the back as Melian welcomed everyone.

"The time has come," she said, "to rebuild our island realm. Not as it was before, but a new era where Apexians and the forest's hidden folk live in harmony." She paused while the significance of her opening statement sank in. "It's time to release the creatures living in our protected forest for five hard years. Our scouting parties tell me Kingstown and Eastport are no-go zones for the hidden folk, Apexians, or wild animals. Everywhere else, the land is coming back to life. Bristlebrink confirms the old forested regions are now safe and will soon regenerate the habitat the animals need."

"But right now," a scout added. "There is little suitable habitat outside the forest we established for the larger animals."

"Not a problem," Melian replied. "We marked off a large area of forest in the days before the chaos and protected it using our magic. We will release the magic spells protecting the area. The animals will continue living there and expand into the remaining forests as they regenerate."

Coggle raised his hand. "Releasing the spells will probably speed up the regeneration process. But what about the Apexians living in the forest?"

"And Bristlebud," Bittybeam added from her seat near the front. "He's dangerous."

"We'll discuss Bristlebud first," Melian replied. "He's reverted to his Apexian form, as he had to after he left the hidden forest. His name's Marc Lebrun. Trouble has followed him wherever he's roamed. We expect nothing different in the future."

"Worse," Dela piped up from her perch near Bittybeam. "We've had him under surveillance since you expelled him from the hidden forest. He left the large animal refuge and joined the fascists in the holiday retreat in the foothills southwest of Kingstown. They plan to eliminate any Apexians who won't join their cause. Coggle may know more."

"Some," Coggle replied. "They have a grandiose scheme to rule the world. Dela called them fascists. That's a good descriptor. They plan to subjugate all Apexians on Neuvo Britannica, then join with like-minded survivors everywhere else, and take over the planet. They won't have sympathy for the forest's hidden folk."

"I agree. They're a serious threat we'll keep under surveillance," Melian said. "That brings me to my last point. We want all our gnomish visitors to resume their Apexian form and return to their world. They could return to the communities where we found them, or anywhere else that offers a chance to rebuild. We will join with them to fend off the fascist threat and produce a new era of collaboration between Apexians and hidden folk on Neuvo Britannica."

"And the alphas in your forest refuge?" Coggle asked. He didn't know how he became the de facto spokesman for the gnomish visitors, but with the aged Bristlebrink unable to get out and about, the leadership role had fallen on his shoulders. "Has Bristlebud's rhetoric influenced their thinking?"

Melian smiled. "Something for you to investigate. Our spy in the animal refuge tells me he got no support. In fact, Bristlebud, I suppose we must get used to calling him Marc Lebrun, didn't willingly leave the refuge. Some may remember Emily Dickson. Dela brought her here in critical condition during the days of chaos, and Iridessa treated her. I'm happy to say she made a complete recovery and became a leader in the refuge. Emily and several of her larger friends threw him out."

Melian then described how they would take the magical energy they'd been devoting to protecting the animal habitat, something they were finding difficult to maintain, and devote their magic to protecting the deserving villages and towns that Rambleroot and his colleagues identified. When the time came, they'd join in the fight to neutralize the rebels in Uplands.

When the meeting broke up, Coggle left with Bittybeam, but his thoughts were on Emily Dickson and how someone as skeptical of the supernatural as Emily became a leader in the refuge.

Melian appeared to be withholding critical information. How could she know it was now safe for her gnomish visitors to return full time to the outside world? What knowledge could she have, and why would she keep it from them? Was she really imagining a future where they work together, or one where both groups were aware of the other, but went their separate ways? Or something more sinister?

17 Survivors on the Outside

Avery Quinn, a young nuclear physicist, machinist, arbalist, and all-round Renaissance man, emerged from his bunker deep underground in the remains of South Serene University's physics building. He'd been alone, monitoring outside conditions from the safety of his underground lair for five years. Radiation levels were less than one per cent of the levels at the height of the civilization-destroying chaos.

This took longer than he expected, suggesting the detonations released longer-lived isotopes than bombs that detonated in the atmosphere. They generated mostly lethal short-lived isotopes.

No country had deployed tactical surface detonating nukes on an unsuspecting population, but their developers knew they'd generate enormous shockwaves of heat and electromagnetic radiation that would incinerate everything for miles around. They would also generate more of those longer-lived isotopes. Whatever the source, it now appeared the world outside his laboratory was safe enough for brief excursions.

He had water and food for another eighteen months. Longer if he could master the decontamination of water from the underground stream he tapped into beneath the building, and his efforts to increase the yield of his hydroponic gardens bore fruit. But after so many months isolated and alone, his curiosity overcame his fears of the unknown world he'd be entering. It was time to get out there and rediscover the outside world. But he wouldn't venture forth without careful planning.

Avery spent the last week before his venture into the great unknown, considering the best route to the surface. He decided, after studying many options, on a narrow shaft with climbing rungs that joined the first and second subterranean levels. He'd determined he could manipulate the hatch at the top. At the bottom, he installed another hatch with a fan that would blow clean air from his laboratory space into the shaft. The rudimentary air exchange system should minimize contamination of his living space.

He'd run out of excuses. Avery grabbed his crossbow and headed for the surface. He took with him a quiver of thirty-six bolts from the extensive supply he'd produced during his isolation.

He climbed a flight of stairs to the sub-basement, one he'd climbed many times during the first months in seclusion. Those were the early days when he used his knowledge of the hidden infrastructure of the university's physics building to force radioactivity probes through electrical conduits to the surface. He had to remove inactive cables to make space for his new ones, but that was no problem. Students installed electrical wires for many experiments, but few removed them after their experiments ended. They could go. He soon had a configuration he could accept. He retreated to subterranean level three to activate his environmental monitoring station.

This time, he took a different route along a corridor to his escape hatch. Avery activated the fan before he closed the lower hatch. He took a deep breath and climbed the ten rungs. He paused just inside the upper hatch, listening for any sign of someone in the area he'd be entering.

An hour later, his muscles ached. He had to either proceed before his muscles seized up completely, or retreat to his lair. He pushed open the hatch and found himself in a storage space cluttered with what looked like useless junk. After wondering for a few minutes what someone used this space for, he decided it was perfect. If he proceeded without disturbing the junk, it would keep his access hatch well hidden.

He stepped around the junk on his way to the doorway. Someone had removed the door, probably to use as fuel for a fire. He peered into the hallway, but saw no one. He paused again, listening, but heard nothing. Debris covered the floor, and many of the walls appeared seriously damaged. He realized that much of the ceiling was gone. Blue sky was visible between the twisted structural beams that once supported the ground floor.

Avery spanned his crossbow and nocked a bolt in the groove. He crept around the larger pieces of debris, climbed a relatively intact stairway to the ground floor and approached what was once the physics building's main entrance.

Outside, he encountered a strange scene. Destroyed or seriously damaged buildings everywhere he looked. The university had been very modern—two- or three-storey glass-clad buildings arranged in concentric circles around the library. At five storeys, it was the tallest building on campus. Now, only a few staircases and twisted metal frameworks that once held the glass panels in place protruded above masses of debris. Trees had blackened trunks with no sign of life, but at ground level, anywhere that had been lawns, flower beds, or foundation plantings were verdant green. Nothing manicured but a thick growth of two-foot-high grasses and weeds battling for space. He imagined mice and perhaps rabbits scurrying about the undergrowth looking for their next meals.

The paved paths between buildings were mostly intact. He wandered along several, keeping his crossbow at the ready in case he noticed a larger, more dangerous animal, or another alpha. After a short, but tense, stroll through the campus, he returned to the physics building and the hatchway to his underground lair.

He noticed her crouching to one side behind some larger chunks of rubble. Instinctively, he raised his crossbow.

"Hi," she said as she stood. "I mean you no harm. Will you please lower that vicious-looking weapon?"

She wasn't a large female and didn't appear armed. If Avery dialled back his mental clock to the days before the conflagration, she could have been an undergraduate student hustling about the campus or loitering in the Student Union Building. He lowered his crossbow but left the bolt nocked.

She stepped out from behind the rubble. "I've known you were down there since I found myself trapped in the basement when the chaos erupted—"

"This building," Avery asked.

She nodded. "I was a biophysics student so often here."

Biophysics meant she was a graduate student, so older than Avery thought. "Sorry I interrupted. Please continue."

"It was black, but I levered away debris until I found a larger space with two walls and part of the ceiling that appeared intact. I collapsed there, exhausted, and when I woke up, I could see light filtering in from the damaged part of the ceiling. I recognized the space—a storage room used by the basement food kiosk—you must remember the place. A godsend because I scrounged four large jugs of water and various foodstuffs that would last me until something happened. I'd either die from radiation poisoning or someone would rescue me."

"But neither happened?"

"Obviously, and I assume your story is similar."

"Similar, maybe, but also different. Like many others who were often disparagingly called survivalists, I expected something catastrophic. I stocked my lab and storage space two floors below this with survival gear and food and water for a long siege. I was studying the radiation effects of what I considered the inevitable thermonuclear war, so I had some idea what to expect."

"But no one can survive global thermonuclear war."

"That's outdated thinking. The modern scenario is regional conflicts with tactical nukes and thermobaric weapons. Such a war should be survivable for sufficiently ruthless aggressors willing to produce enormous numbers of casualties."

"So you were prepared and planning to wait it out. Do you have radiation monitors that now tell you it's safe?"

He shook his head. "I do, but they're obviously too conservative. You've been spending time outside and survived."

"I was worried sick for months when I ventured outside. But I had no choice. My food supply dwindled, and it was find more food or starve." She reached back into her hiding place, where she extracted two small carcasses. "Thinking of which, would you like to share spit roasted rabbits with me for supper?"

"Or would you rather visit my refuge where we could prepare rabbit stew with mushrooms and green onions and any other veggies I can scare up? Probably healthier than your regular fare."

18 Life at the university

In Avery's refuge, the browned rabbit meat was soon simmering in water on his hotplate. Akari, for that was the name she gave him, was pedaling his exercise bike to generate electricity to replenish an array of storage batteries. The name he guessed was Nihonese, which was consistent with her oriental appearance.

"Is this how you generate the electricity you need for your underground wonder-world?" she asked as she abandon his bike and slumped into an easy chair.

He laughed. "Small experimental nuclear power plant generates all the power I need with masses to spare. If conditions stabilize, it could supply power for 1000 people."

"Then what's with the bike?"

"It's my exercise bike, but I'm happier if I'm doing something useful as I pedal. You offered to take a turn."

"Kuso!" she said as she jumped off the bike. "I thought I was helping cook our dinner."

He watched her chopping up vegetables and fussing with the stew as he pedalled his bike. When she turned away from the hotplate, he stopped pedalling. "I could string a cable from the reactor to your hideout. You could have light and a hotplate if we can find one."

She shook her head. "Dangerous. A light would be visible from outside. It could attract unwelcome visitors."

He abandoned the bike. Her statements were inconsistent. A fire she used to spit roast rabbits would attract more unwanted visitors than a single light bulb. Or would it? A fire would suggest another refugee from the conflagration, but electric lights would suggest technology. That could be a significant difference.

"Have you seen other people or large predators?" he asked.

"The rabbit population is expanding, so I expect very few predators, even small ones like foxes. And as for others like us, I've known you were down here, but I couldn't find my way in."

"How did you know I was down here?"

"Noises. I heard noises that couldn't be random. There had to be someone living on a deeper level."

"But no one outside while you were hunting or whatever?"

"I've seen no one since I hiked to Eastport in the early days…"

She paused with a few tears welling in her eyes, obviously lost in thoughts of a frightening visit. After several minutes, she rubbed her eyes.

"Bombs levelled the entire town, much more seriously damaged than our campus and the village just beyond. I saw some survivors. At first, I thought they were zombies or other malevolent creatures from horror movies I watched back home in Edo. I laid low and watched, probably longer than I should have because radiation levels must have been high. I decided their brains were so damaged by the radiation, they could do nothing but stumble through the rubble, searching for anything edible. They really looked like zombies from second-rate horror movies."

Avery wandered to his workbench and shuffled through some rolled-up papers on the shelf underneath. He pulled out four as Akari peered over his shoulder. Avery spread out the topmost one. "This is a map of our area before the chaos, with the Eastport near the top, and the airport, more or less to the west." He tapped an area 60 kilometres southeast of the port city. "We're here on the side of the region's largest lake. Forest surrounds the campus and its village. Farther west, the forests yield to more cultivated land and off the map's upper left side, we have Kingstown."

"I can tell you the forest and the wooden buildings in our village are burnt to cinders, and I saw no surviving trees between here and our little fishing port. Just grasses and weeds poking through the ground."

He placed another map next to the first. "This is the after picture, darker hash marking where the destruction was greatest. Black where nuclear explosions dominated grading into red areas where thermobaric explosions generated wildfires."

"How can you know this if you never left your bunker until today?"

"A lot of speculation, but I have continuous radiation level measurements from a single ground level monitoring station directly above us. We also know that electronic communication from around the world has gone completely dead."

"So, you're speculating tactical nukes blasted Eastport, the airport, and the regional capital off the northwestern corner of your map. Elsewhere, fires supported by the blast from the thermobaric weapons burned everything. I can believe that. When tons of rubble trapped me for several days one floor below ground, I thought I was going to die from the heat. I can't imagine how I survived, but where's this leading us?"

Avery placed another map next to the first two. Graphs displaying changes in radioactivity versus time at various locations adorned it. "The port, the airport, and the capital will remain seriously contaminated with the heavier isotopes that became attached to the soils. The lighter airborne isotopes were very high at first, but they've decreased quickly. Give them a few more months…"

"A few more months, and then what?"

"We'll be able to leave our underground bunkers and rebuild a new village on an open part of the university campus."

"Why not farther away, far from those radiation hotspots?"

"Because we'd want it close enough to my reactor to supply electricity to the houses."

A few minutes later, Akari wandered over and gave her stew a stir. "Looking good. It will soon be ready to eat. Now if only we had some potatoes. We'd have a perfect feast."

"Spuds! No problem. My hydroponics garden works for spuds. They're kinda small, but they're tasty, and you don't have to peel them."

She turned to Avery. "Like really, can we boil a few?"

He marched out and returned moments later with a large handful of potatoes. They were all roughly five centimetres in diameter. "Your wish is my command." He quartered them and placed them in a pot before reaching into the cupboards under his cooking area for a second hotplate. He set everything up with a flourish.

"Amazing! You must show me all your marvels."

When she turned the heat down to simmer, he pointed down a dimly lit hallway. "Not the reactor. Locked door with various levels of security designed to isolate any radiation if we have a problem."

"Where's your garden? You obviously grow mushrooms, carrots, green onions, and potatoes."

"This way," he said as he pushed his stool away from the counter that did double duty as a cooking and eating area. He led her past food storage bins on both sides of a short passageway to another door. When he opened it, intense light produced by banks of bulbs blasted them. "Hydroponics on the right, regular greenhouse on the left, and mushrooms at floor level in an area that only gets dim light. I'll leave you to explore while I check on the stew."

When she returned, Akari was bright-eyed with excitement. "I have it figured out," she said. "I move my refuge from the partial basement where

69

it now is to one floor down. That makes it one floor above this one. Right?" She paused, giving her stew a final stir. "You can run a cable to that space so I can have lights and enough electricity for a hotplate, assuming I can find one, without producing light that attracts unwanted visitors. When the radiation drops to acceptable levels, we can dig up all the weeds on what was the university's lawns and gardens, and start growing veggies outside. When we want to attract the attention of others who might join us in building a community, you can wire up a light in the wreckage of a building. If there's anyone out there, they'll see it and come exploring."

"Makes sense because I was having difficulty figuring out how we would generate the building materials we'd need for houses."

"When do we start?"

"Once we've eaten. You can start by finding the space you want to claim as your own."

19 An Outside Threat

After Akari Yamada climbed the ladder to his escape hatch and strode away from her 'dinner date' with Avery, she had much to consider. Her bosses had chosen her for the mission based on her survival skills and her knowledge of Britannican. She now had a problem. Like everyone else, she harboured secrets.

The first was her short-wave radio. She couldn't admit she had it with her in the physics building, listening for signals from Nihon when the disaster struck. Her fire and-bomb-proof strong box with its radiation meter and supply of radiation exposure pills was more problematical. She'd rescued the box from the rubble that was her university residence and lugged it to her physics building hide-away. How could she explain this gear and maintain the pretense of being an innocent biophysics student?

Her last secret, a cache of high-powered weapons, would be even harder to explain. Fortunately, the cache was secure. It had a detector that would send a message to her radio if anything disturbed it. Nothing had messed with it in five years. She'd recently checked on it without approaching too closely. It was okay. *Should I tell Avery about them?*

She had secrets, but Avery must have his own. Had he been in his bunker for five years without once venturing outside? Or was he one of a team responsible for keeping the reactor going? If he was a team-member, where were the others, and why were they keeping the reactor running?

On a more personal note, she wondered about Avery's reaction when she admitted she'd been watching for him. He accepted that revelation with a shrug, and treated the whole encounter, including her visit to his lab, like she was a tourist visiting an interesting research facility. But he said he'd seen no one for five years. What made him so standoffish? You'd think thoughts of others in their realm and the possibility of building a community would have engaged his mind.

The next morning, Akari snuck outside to check her snares. They were all empty. Time to find another area with good rabbit habitat. She could set up there and let the closer to home population rebuild and forget about avoiding snares.

Her new insights into the relative safety in the outside environment had her searching for evidence of alphas or larger animals. She found no signs of larger animals or alphan visitors, but her trained senses picked up indications of rabbits a few hundred metres from her older hunting grounds.

After setting her snares, she picked berries and dug up a few wild carrots on her way back to her lair. Until her new snares started catching rabbits, she'd have a limited diet. Nothing new. She'd lived through lean spells in the past, and she had her fishing line and her bow and arrows to fall back on. Until now, she avoided fishing or bow hunting because it meant staying outside for longer periods, but Avery convinced her the risks were now minimal. *I'd bloody well better make it work because I refuse to contemplate becoming reliant on Avery Quinn for food. Electricity, yes, but not food, unless I've something useful to trade.*

Days later, she'd commandeered her new living space, one level lower than her previous lair, but close to it with a navigable back stairway that was hard to find. Avery connected it to his power source, and she now had two lamps and electricity for cooking. It was less exposed to residual radiation and safer for sleeping. But she preferred her other digs with their glimpse of the sky through the damaged ceiling and her spit for roasting rabbits.

She set off at dawn to explore the river draining into the lake near the university and try her luck at fishing. Fish would expand her diet that was far too dependent on rabbits and berries.

The fishing was good. She started home shortly before the sun was overhead with four brown trout. Along the way, she noticed several boot prints in muddy ground near a stream draining into the river. They weren't there when she passed the same spot in the morning. Two individuals, maybe three, she thought as she abandoned the open ground into rougher terrain that contained rubble from damaged buildings and larger bramble bushes that would offer camouflage.

She stopped when she heard voices and dived behind a thick berry producing bramble.

"That idiot with tales of elves and fairies and alphas transforming into gnomes is off his bloody rocker. There's nothing here but burnt-out forest and rubble from that disgusting socialist university," said one voice.

"He's a smooth-talking bastard who has the leader's ear. We shouldn't cross him. Be careful about what you say about him."

"Physics building, he said. How the hell are we supposed to find the physics building in all this bloody rubble?"

"The research wing, not the teaching facilities."

"Bloody hell. I couldn't identify any buildings in all this mess, and he wants us to find a particular wing of a particular building! What's so bloody special about it, anyway?"

"A nuclear reactor that could provide power for a new headquarters for our movement. We can't subjugate survivors unless we're reaching out from a position of strength. Power from a nuclear reactor gives us that leverage."

"Bollocks! Nuclear bombs destroyed everything. Now you tell me a nuclear power reactor will give us the advantage we need to subjugate the survivors."

"Forget the bloody politics. Just follow me. I can find the physics building and the wing with the reactor. We confirm it's still functional and get the hell out of here."

Akari remained hidden, gorging on berries until they returned. She didn't have long to wait. They were, as Akari guessed from the boot prints in the mud, members of a vigilante army in military fatigues.

"So, you think the idiot with his fairy tales is right? We heard functioning machinery, but how do we know it's a reactor?"

"Trust me. I was a student here and knew about the reactor. I dropped out because I couldn't stand the woke political correctness and their disdain for libertarian ideas. The rumbling was in the right place, and it makes sense. If someone could keep a reactor going, it gives him power."

"Power we need."

"You got it. Power we need. Let's get moving. We've seen no one, but who knows how many sentinels they have out here looking for the likes of us?"

Akari waited in her hiding place until they were out of hearing before making a careful approach to her new lair. She left her fish there before going to warn Avery.

20 Arrivals from the Hidden Forest

Ethan Johnson, known for five years by his gnomish name Coggle, Keilani Alana, previously known as Bittybeam, and four other gnomes recently returned to their alphan form, arrived at South Serene University. Dela and her team of fairies sped them on their journey, but when they reached the university, the fairies vanished. They remained in the immediate vicinity, but invisible.

Ethan approached the standpipe with the sensors from Avery's underground lab. He banged on the side of the hard, fire resistant, plastic conduit to attract the attention of anyone waiting below ground, then retreated from the physics building.

A crossbowman appeared in the doorway ten minutes later. He had a bolt nocked on his weapon and appeared ready to fire. "I'm Avery Quinn, and who, pray tell, are you?"

"Ethan Johnson at your service, and please, have patience," Ethan said. "We come in peace and wish you no harm. We have a strange tale to tell and an important warning for you."

When Avery made no move to lower his weapon, Dela appeared from behind him and removed the bolt from its nocked position. She handed it to him.

"How the hell did you do that?" he exclaimed. Avery, like any arbalist, knew one cannot simply remove a nocked bolt. "And who the hell are you?"

"Dela, one of the hidden folk in the southern forest. If you don't put down that weapon, I'll take it from you."

Avery hesitated for a few seconds too long. The crossbow flew from his hands to Dela's. She stared at it for a few moments, then flew off and handed it to Ethan.

The commotion brought Akari and two others from the shadows. They went to stand with Avery.

"That," Ethan said, without acknowledging the three new alphas, "should make our strange tale more believable." He introduced Dela and her winged compatriots, and described their lives with the elves, fairies, and gnomes in the hidden forest. "The reason," he concluded, "for the

74

theatrical performance is quite simple. The six of us," he said, pointing at Keilani and their four alphan companions, "wish to return to live here in harmony with you and any others living in the broader university community. You will need us, and the magic provided by our friends from the hidden forest."

"And why's that?" Avery interjected.

"Because of the threat I mentioned a few minutes ago. There is only one alphan community on Neuvo Britannica that's large enough and belligerent enough to generate a problem. They have their sights set on taking over your reactor. You'll need defenders and probably the forest folk's magic to fend off the vigilante army amassing far to the west in the mountain foothills. They're armed, dangerous, and won't listen to logical arguments. You must be prepared to defeat them."

"Garbage," Avery replied. "You have a very realistic-looking fairy drone and some slick technology. This doesn't fool me."

"I've been to Uplands, as has Dela," Ethan replied, pointing to the fairy still hovering above him. "We heard the bellicose rhetoric and threats from their leader. They're a serious problem and you—we—must resist them."

The oriental-looking woman standing with Avery touched his shoulder to get his attention. "Remember the interlopers I saw a few weeks ago? Could they have been an advance party, here to assess our defensive capacity?"

"Shh, Akari," Avery whispered. "We mustn't give anything away."

Dela dropped to the ground and transformed into an Apexian dressed in military fatigues like the ones she'd seen in their foray into the vigilantes' mountain headquarters. "Well, Akari, were they dressed like this and interested in your reactor?"

"Kuso," Akari whispered. "They know my name and exactly how those visitors looked."

"Anything else," Ethan said, "we must do to convince you our fairy companions are real and that we come in peace?"

One of Avery's compatriots, a male, stepped forward. "My name's George Brown and my infant daughter's sickly. Can you do anything to help her?"

Iridessa, a constant member of Dela's team, flew forward. "I'm a healer. Show me the way and I'll do what I can." She followed him into the remains of the physics building with another fairy behind her, watching for any belligerent moves.

Avery and his two remaining companions stood at the top of the physics building steps, and Ethan and his friends waited on the path leading to the steps. No one in either group uttered a word.

Iridessa returned ten minutes later, with George huffing away just behind her. "It's a miracle," he said. "She's breathing better, smiling, and playing with Faye, the other fairy. I haven't seen Audrey, Emma, or Mia so happy in well, a very long time."

"Not cured," Iridessa replied. "I've eased her pain and given her extra strength to fight off the infection. The rest is up to Mia."

"And Faye?" Dela asked.

"She's made some new friends. You know how much she likes the little ones."

Over the next few minutes, the tension between the two groups decreased, but only a little. Then Faye flew from the building with Mia clinging to her shoulders, chortling the way happy infants do. Audrey and Emma emerged close behind.

"More fairies!" Emma yelled when she saw Dela and the rest of the team. "Isn't it wonderful?" She bounded down the stairs and reached up, trying to grab one. The fairy flew away, but only a few metres, and Emma chased after her.

Mia squirmed, and Faye landed on the path near Ethan and Keilani. Mia ignored them as she toddled after her sister.

"It really is amazing," George said as he watched his younger daughter's antics. "We must organize a feast to welcome our new residents and their fairy host that's so enraptured our kids."

And so it came to pass. Ethan, Keilani, and four other alphas found new homes in subbasements of mostly destroyed university buildings. Their acceptance doubled the adult population of University. They'd soon converted sizeable areas tucked away behind the university buildings into vegetable gardens. Their fishing and hunting parties and scavengers for berries and edible plants produced food for all. They ventured forth in teams of three or four, always watching for vigilantes approaching from the west.

21 Imminent Battle

Weeks later, Ethan and Keilani, with Akari standing guard, were expanding a garden they'd planted after they arrived. The compost piles they generated were festering nicely, albeit pungently, making up for the lack of commercial fertilizer in their post-apocalyptic world. Their gardening tools were simple, many produced by Avery in his little machine shop, and others scrounged from the debris that was the nearby town. Progress was both hard work and slow.

They didn't notice the bear until it was quite close. "Excuse me, Ethan," it said as it reared up on its hind legs. "Sorry to interrupt your work expanding the rabbit's food supply, but I have an important message for you and everyone else in your little community."

All three dropped their tools, and Akari shrieked. The return of the talking bear was not a complete surprise to Ethan, and five years living in the hidden forest prepared Keilani for strange new encounters with fantastical creatures, but for Akari, it was a novel experience.

"So, we meet again," Ethan replied. "Our previous communication didn't result in a positive outcome? Something more positive this time?"

"A warning. An armed party of fifty marauders from Uplands, the holiday resort in the western mountains, is a day's march from here. They intend to take your community by force. Whether my message is positive or negative news depends on how you react." The bear turned, dropped back onto all four legs, and ambled a few metres before turning its massive head. "A contingent of fairies will arrive at dawn to help with your defence."

"Is that for real?" Akari asked as they watched the bear disappear behind a higher pile of rubble.

"Definitely," Keilani replied. "That bear is actually an elf from the hidden forest, bringing us a message we cannot ignore."

An hour later, the eighteen residents of their little community gathered to discuss the depressing news. Only George and Audrey's older daughter, Emma, saw the positive side. "Will Faye be back to play with us?"

"I hope so," Avery replied. "But first we must chase away some bad guys. You, Mia, and your mother must stay in your underground rooms until they're gone. Promise me you won't come up looking for Faye. It won't be safe for you or for Faye."

Emma nodded, but everyone could tell from her expression that she was very disappointed. Life with only her baby sister to play with and so many warnings about her safety was difficult for a young girl with so few toys who wanted to explore her world.

After Audrey, Emma, and Mia retreated to a back corner of the room, Avery got down to the serious business of their meeting. "I have three extra crossbows. George, Matthew, and Akari have been practicing. We should resume that practice today and invite our newcomers to join us."

George held up his hand. "Matt and I have hunting rifles, but not enough ammo for an extended battle."

Avery turned to Ethan, who'd been watching Akari. Her furtive looks suggested she had something to hide. "Any weapons?" Avery asked.

"One hunting rifle amongst us, but like George said, insufficient ammunition for a serious encounter."

"So that's where we stand," Avery said. "Today we practice with the crossbows and get a feel for their range. Tomorrow, we stay hidden until the invaders come into crossbow range. We must identify their leaders and target them with all we've got. It's our only hope."

Ethan watched Akari depart and nodded to Keilani, who followed at a distance. He waited with the other alphas from the hidden forest for his lesson in crossbow operation.

Keilani followed Akari, keeping well back because there was little cover. Akari descended the rough footpath to the lake and strode along the shore for four or five hundred metres. There she waited, perched on a flat rock for Keilani to catch up.

"Saw you following me," Akari said. "Better you than someone else, because I need your advice."

"What sort of advice?"

Akari pointed at the lake. "I have a stash in a waterproof bag with a rope coil that will extend to the shore. I need to retrieve it before tomorrow."

"Someone needs to dive to get to it?"

Akari nodded. "I can do that, but I'll need a boat to raise the bag. If I drag it ashore, I'm afraid I'll cause a leak. Water will ruin everything."

"So a boat or a raft you can float out to it. How far? Like the middle of the lake?"

"Ten metres offshore and four metres deep."

"Where do I come into this?"

"Can your fairies produce a boat?"

Keilani shook her head. "Not sure, but they're stronger than us. If they had your rope and the sediment hadn't buried the package, they could lift it."

"Great," Akari replied as she shed her clothes. "You conjure up your fairies while I retrieve my rope and make sure the bag is sitting on top of the sediment."

"No wait. I can't just conjure them up. They'll be here at dawn. Won't that do?"

Akari stood, her head tilted to one side, for a few seconds. "Yeah, fine. I'll retrieve the rope and make sure the package is free. You produce some fairies tomorrow, as early as possible."

She turned and strode into the water until it was neck deep, then submerged. She came up for air several times before swimming back, trailing an algae-covered rope. Akari secured the free end under a rock a metre from shore and sat on her rock, leaning back for maximum exposure to the sun. "That water is cold."

The next day, before dawn, Dela and another fairy appeared in the rooms Keilani shared with Ethan.

"What's up?" Ethan asked as he rubbed the sleep from his eyes. "Are they here already?"

"Camped a two-hour march from here," Dela replied. "Haryk's watching them, and another contingent of fairies is approaching. We're here early because Keilani requested our help. Iridessa and Faye are also here to check on Mia's progress."

Ethan blinked, realizing Keilani was already dressed. "Why?"

"Not sure. It's Akari who needs their help."

"And who's Haryk?" Ethan asked as Keilani neared the door.

"An elf. Melian's second in command."

"The bear!" Ethan exclaimed to the empty room. *Haryk must be the bear who appeared at my forest study site before the chaos, and the one who arrived yesterday to warn us about the impending battle.*

22 The Big Battle

Keilani picked her way down the rock-strewn path to the lake in the dawn's early light. Dela and her friend flew alongside, uninhibited by any ground-level obstructions. Akari waited on her flat rock with the algae-covered rope in her hand.

Dela took it from Akari and stared at it for several minutes. The algae on the first three or four metres shrivelled up, leaving the rope dirty, but not slick and slimy. "Better," she said. "It will now be easier to grip. What do you want us to do? Fly out 'till we're above your package, pull it straight up and bring it back here?" When Akari nodded, Dela added, "okay if we bring it back in the water? That makes it lighter, less of a lift."

Akari nodded again. "Provided you don't drag it on the bottom."

Dela flew out, gaining height as she went until she reached the spot directly above Akari's package. The other fairy gripped the rope, and they flew upwards until the package broke the surface. Then it was only a few seconds back to shore where they hovered with Akari's package above the water at the shoreline. They made the job look easy, but when Akari struggled to lift it onto the beach, Keilani realized it was anything but easy.

Akari checked the seals and when she knew it was dry, the two fairies grabbed the handholds on each side of the large carryall and flew it up to the physics building. When Akari and Keilani arrived, they found all the adults except Audrey assembled, discussing strategy.

Avery stared at the slimy kitbag for several seconds. "What's that?" he demanded. "And why have you kept it hidden from us? Somewhere underwater, obviously."

"It contains ten semiautomatic rifles and lots of ammunition. Also, emergency medical supplies. Stuff we'll need today, so I retrieved it. I'll explain later. There's not time right now."

Their enemy arrived on the outskirts of the university when the sun was about halfway from the horizon to its peak elevation, so about 9 a.m. They stopped in an area beyond the working range of a standard hunting rifle, where dead trees and living brush offered them some cover, waiting for a horse-drawn cart to catch up.

80

Ethan watched the cart as they pulled it up to their rendezvous point, fearing it might contain an artillery piece, but he couldn't see one. *Is it just food and other supplies for the attack force? Or does it contain something more lethal?*

He counted heads and came up with fifty, the number the bear gave them, but only half were carrying rifles. The rest had wooden spears and war clubs from centuries earlier.

A few minutes later, they started marching forward. They had fifty, twenty-five with single shot hunting rifles, against five defenders of the front of the building because Avery had deployed three alphas and three fairies to defend the sides and back, but they were all well hidden and seven had modern semiautomatic weapons.

"What do we do?" Keilani asked, touching the semiautomatic Ethan had trained on the vigilante in the centre of the invading group. He appeared in charge and looked like the leader who's meeting he'd snuck into back in his Coggle days.

"I think the guy in the centre is their leader, and the one with the crazy helmet with the spike on top could be Marc Lebrun. Melian said his gnomish name was Bristlebud."

"I think so. If your old friend Emily was here, she would know."

"Can't help it. We'll go with our impression. Tell Avery we should take out those two. Akari can take their leader and I'll take Bristlebud, and remind everyone, single shot mode. We don't want them to know we have semis."

Keilani hustled away and returned at almost exactly the time when the invaders stopped only one hundred metres from their hiding places. They were sitting ducks.

Before she could speak, the invaders' leader stepped forward and yelled through a bullhorn. "Put down whatever weapons you have and raise a white flag. If you join us, we'll be an unassailable force, one that can rule our island for generations to come. You have two minutes to raise a flag. If not, we'll charge your positions and take you by force. We'll spare no one."

In the silence that followed, Keilani whispered. "Avery agrees with your plan. I'm off to tell Akari, and Audrey is reminding the others about using single shot mode."

"What about Emma and Mia? If they show their faces, it could ruin everything."

"No worry, Faye's looking after them. She won't let anyone harm them."

"Good. Safer than we could keep them. Now, get the word to Akari. You've only got a minute."

She hurried away, and when the invaders' leader raised his hand to start the charge, a single shot rang out and he dropped to the ground. A flurry of shots from the other defenders hit a few others. Ethan steadied his rifle, took careful aim, and squeezed the trigger. Bristlebud, Marc Lebrun, or whoever he was, dropped like a stone. Ethan sighed. He'd just killed his first alpha. He hoped he'd never have to kill another.

Seven invaders were lying on the ground, some motionless, others in distress. The other invaders broke ranks. Six laid their guns on the ground, raised their hands, and joined six others walking forward with their hands raised. The rest ran away.

Avery called out, "Cease firing."

The battle was over only seconds after it started.

Fairies appeared from their hiding places. Some, led by Iridessa, applied first aid to the wounded, others collected the abandoned weapons, and a third contingent followed the retreating invaders. Two returned a few minutes later, standing on the backs of the horses, pulling the invaders' supply cart. "Look what they left behind?" one said. They obviously loved the way their fairy magic played an undisclosed role in their liberation of the cart and its two draft horses.

Akari joined Iridessa, and they set up a field hospital on the portico of the physics building to treat the wounded. Avery, George, and two others took charge of their twelve captives. Faye released Emma and Mia from their confinement underground, and the victory party of alphas and fairies lasted into the evening.

23 The Next Days

Ethan woke up nestled against Keilani in their tiny underground space in the university's physics building. So much had changed in the days since they prepared to leave the hidden forest. He lay there thinking about it.

The first significant step occurred the morning before they transformed back into Apexian form, when Coggle gave Fidgow in marriage to Rambleroot. That joyous event included the transfer of ownership of his gnomish cottage to Fidgow and Rambleroot. It was followed by a second, more hastily arranged marriage.

Coggle and Bittybeam joined their hands in gnomish matrimony. The legality of the ceremony after they returned to alphan form may have been questionable, but neither was worried. They were unlikely to find preachers after they returned to the outside world. A gnomish marriage was their only choice, and they cherished the idea. It was a unique union sanctioned by a magical society that saved their lives five years earlier and provided a fulfilling existence during the intervening pentade.

On the morning after the battle, when Ethan and Keilani reached the lobby of the physics building—a mostly cleaned out area that had turned into an informal gathering place—they encountered Avery and Akari in a heated argument. Avery turned to the two newcomers. "Did you know what she was doing?"

Ethan simply shook his head, but Keilani took a more aggressive stance. "Knew nothing until yesterday when Akari asked me to help her, but you should be thankful. She saved us from a very bloody confrontation and possibly the loss of our independence."

Avery didn't back down. "I accept that, but it's not the point. She's a spy for some Nihonese aggressors who planned to take over our island."

"We did not! I was an agent sent here by owners of two small deep-sea fishing companies based in Edo to pave the way for a request to move their operations to Neuvo Britannica if we encountered the chaos we did five years ago. No different from you," Akari continued, pointing a gesticulating finger at Avery. "You also predicted this disaster and set up your operation in the subbasement."

"Not the same," Avery shot back. "I handled reactor operations, so I had a right to be here. I added the underground greenhouse to provide the food I needed to support my duties. The reactor benefits any survivors, and it's a threat to no one."

"So, what's the big difference? Our fishing fleet is offshore vessels. Neuvo Britannica's fishing industry is inshore. No conflict there, and if we moved our processing to Eastport, it would be good for Neuvo Britannica."

"So why the automatic weapons?"

"Defence. For use only if we encountered the very situation we faced yesterday."

"But your plans didn't work," Ethan said to diffuse the situation.

Akari shook her head. "Four offshore fishing boats left Idopoto four days before the chaos erupted. They were well offshore, should have been safe, but radio communication ceased abruptly and I've heard nothing since."

"Massive electromagnetic pulses," Avery said. "Tactical nukes, thermobaric weapons, suddenly enhanced global warming, and now massive electromagnetic pulses. The complete destruction of all modern technology is becoming clearer." He turned and left the lobby.

"Does that mean he accepts my arguments?" Akari asked.

"Who knows," Keilani replied, "but we should assume so until we learn otherwise. Now, what about your medical treatment of our captives?"

Akari sighed. "Iridessa and I did what we could. Three were dead in the field. A fourth died despite our efforts after we got him here. The remaining three are recovering. Iridessa is looking after them."

"And where are our other captives?" Ethan asked.

"George has them in a field behind the chemistry building. They're building a paddock for the horses using stone walls for fencing."

Several days later, Haryk returned in his elfin form, not masquerading as a bear or another fearsome creature. He addressed a crowd that had grown to twenty-five adults and two small children.

"We've subdued the resistance led by two individuals in the aggressors' mountain retreat. The rest were unwilling conscripts shanghaied into the service of the despot you killed four days ago. Many had wives and children who were being held captive to keep their husbands in line. That is over. They know the hidden forest exists and that we offer cooperation with all Apexians who maintain peaceful relations with other Apexians.

Most of the residents are returning with their families to their towns and villages. Some are heading this way, including one family with grown children and a flock of sheep. We trust you'll welcome them."

"How do you know the resistors won't return to their antisocial behaviour?" Ethan asked.

"Fairies and elves will stay out of sight, but keep any resistors at bay."

"What about Bristlebrink?" Keilani asked.

"Ah, Bristlebrink," Haryk replied. "He and Mildred have remained as gnomes in our forest. His health is improving, less stress, I'd say. They'd welcome brief visits from old friends if you're interested."

Keilani glanced at Ethan. "Will that be possible?"

Haryk nodded. "Get a message to Aurora. She'll work something out." He hesitated, gazing at the various faces. "I must submit my report to Melian. Before I do, I should reiterate what we've said in all towns and villages. Live in peace, and the elves, fairies, and gnomes will have your backs."

He waved to everyone before turning and walking away. A mist descended on the grounds, and when it lifted, he was gone, replaced by ten alphas and a small flock of bleating sheep coming their way.

In less than an hour, Haryk was presenting his report to Melian. "All is in place for a new golden age in our homeland, or as the Apexians call it, Neuvo Britannica. They are now aware of our presence and our role in keeping the peace. It's a new world for everyone."

"But what about rebels unreceptive to our forward-looking ideas?" Melian asked.

"Heading for Kingstown. They'll find an empty wasteland that remains toxic. It has no recruits for any effort to cause further mayhem, and if they linger too long, the residual radiation will do them in."

"That leaves us with only one immediate problem—my stubborn brother and his two followers. Intevar and Connak have both rejected my suggestion they return to the hidden forest. They prefer to live out their lives as Apexians. Sylvar seemed more receptive to my offer but worried about abandoning Intevar."

"May I make a suggestion," Haryk said.

"By all means. Making suggestions when I'm stumped is your job."

"We install Connak, Rory MacGregor to the Apexians, a cautious individual who can be one tough customer when necessary, as the new leader of the mountain retreat's remaining residents."

"An odd choice," Melian said, "but he's restless and herding those sheep wastes his talents. I see how it could work for him and the residents of Uplands. That leaves Sylvar."

"If you agree, I'll approach Connak about a role that should appeal to him. I'll leave Sylvar to you."

"And the Apexians in our animal refuge?"

"Small groups left for their homes in fishing villages on the southeast coast. They should be home by now. Two larger groups are preparing to leave for University and Uplands. They have far to go, so their journeys will take some time. The last group wishes to stay where they are."

"Let them stay, at least for now. They can assume responsibility for Intevar's sheep. We no longer need those stupid animals, because we no longer need to remain hidden from the Apexians. Still have the same job for Sylvar—my eyes and ears searching for Apexian activity on far off continents. That leaves my annoying brother. What do we do with him?"

"You must convince him to return to the Hidden Forest. Leaving him on the outside as a lone elf, or as the Apexians would say, a lone wolf, is not a good idea, and you know he was right about establishing links with trustworthy Apexians."

Melian sighed. "You're right, as usual, but he's so damned annoying."

24 Saying Goodbye to their Refuge

A week earlier, Emily Dickson returned from her regular visit to check on Noah MacGregor's flock late in the afternoon of a sunny day. The ewes were thriving, and the survival rate for this spring's lambs was the best she'd witnessed in four years ministering to the fluffy little darlings. Even the crotchety old shepherd admitted he'd never seen so many frolicking lambs.

Their settlement within the animal's refuge was abuzz with animated conversation. Don sought her out, as he often did after her visits to the shepherd's croft.

"Joan's received another of her messages from beyond," he said as he followed her to her bamboo house. "This one said we should prepare ourselves to leave the refuge within thirty days."

"One month's notice before we're evicted. Did she say where we should go?"

"Yes."

"Well..."

"To the communities we escaped from."

"Why?"

"To restart Apexian communities."

"Did she actually say Apexian, rather than alphan?"

"Yes."

"Interesting," Emily said, frowning. "More evidence Joan's in communication with the mysterious force guiding our lives for the last five years. What can it mean? Some can return to places they considered their homes, but others, like you, you can't return. Kingstown, if we trust everything we've learned, will be a hotbed of radiation. And for me, home is across the Serene Sea in North Columbia, the North Columbian Union. How do I get there?"

"They probably expect you to return to University."

"Perhaps, but wouldn't it make sense to stick together, establish the best destination and all go there?"

"That place would probably be University."

Emily's frown turned into a smile. "If that's your opinion, can I assume you'd accompany me on my trek, even if others won't?"

Discussion of moving on after five years in the animal refuge dominated the discussion over the following days. Two groups, fisherfolk in their earlier lives, returned to their tiny fishing harbours on the southeast coast. Everything they'd learned over five long years suggested the southeast coast was not too far away. They left before their month's notice expired.

When they learned Noah, Rory, and Harris had abandoned his sheep and shelties, another group, farmers and shepherds in their previous lives, said they'd remain in the refuge. They'd take over Noah's flock and dogs, as well as any remaining chickens and goats. They'd move farther down the mountain if the mysterious entities telling them they had to leave insisted they do so. Joan Jessup, who always seemed to know more than she revealed, led that group.

The remaining groups faced longer treks, so needed longer to prepare. On the thirtieth day, Emily and her group of fourteen bid adieu to the remaining thirty-four alphas in the animal forest and set off for University. The last group of ten planned to leave in the coming days. Their destination was Uplands, the mountain resort to the southwest of Kingstown.

Emily and Don departed with five other adults and seven youngsters on a sunny early summer morning. They carried most of their possessions, food for what they expected to be a fourteen-day journey, and two crates of chickens. With all that baggage and several small children, progress was slow.

Their plan was simple, but seemed as foolproof as they could make it. They'd travel in a roughly eastward direction until they encountered the East River. Then they'd follow the river downstream until they found a suitable place for a few days' rest and replenishment of their food supplies. During that time, they'd send scouts to determine the best route to their next resting place. They'd move forward in three-or-four-day marches, followed by a few days' rest. It was their only choice, given how loaded down they were.

On the second day at their first rest stop, a woman who hadn't previously been outside their protected forest accompanied Emily and a cluster of children in search of berries and other edible plants. "I didn't know how desolated it was," she said. "Blackened tree trunks everywhere we look. It's been the same since we left our refuge."

"Better now than two years ago," Emily replied. "The ground was as black and bleak as the tree stumps. Now we have bushes and grasses and other ground cover." Emily stopped and pointed for the children's sake at a bush loaded with red berries. It was early for blackberries, but it had a nice sunny location. "Remember," she yelled as the kids scampered off, "only pick the black ones. The red ones aren't ready yet."

After the kids with their pails, and the adult woman to ride herd on them, departed, Emily focused on her search for fennel, nasturtiums, banana passion fruit, and onion weed. Anything she could find to liven up the dried food they'd brought with them. Others were out again, trying their luck at fishing. If everyone was successful, they could have a feast.

Robbie MacRae returned from his scouting trip as the sun was setting. He was another refugee from University, a born wanderer who knew more about their route than anyone else. He plunked himself on a blackened log beside Emily and Dan. "Found a suitable destination for our next bivouac. It's by a pool on a tributary of the river. Should be good fishing and lots of greenery for your foraging."

"We'd appreciate better fishing," Emily said as a berry picker from that afternoon's efforts brought her father a bowl of stew. "We have blackberries for dessert," the child said.

"Why don't you share my portion with your little brother?" Robbie replied. "Would you like that?" The girl smiled before scurrying away.

"We've had no success with our fishing efforts," Emily said. "Too fast flowing, apparently. But how far is it?"

"Two days at a pace the youngsters can manage. I say we get on with it."

Don glanced at Emily, who nodded. He rose from his perch on a flat rock. "I'll tell everyone we're heading out tomorrow morning after an early breakfast."

One evening, a month after they left their refuge, Robbie returned from his latest scouting trip with good news. "I've been close enough to the university to assess the situation. It looks good, at least thirty alphas, adult males and females, plus many youngsters. They have two horses, many sheep and chickens, extensive vegetable gardens, and even a few flower beds. The only odd thing is a lack of houses. I didn't see a single house."

In mid-afternoon two days later, Emily's scraggly band of trekkers arrived outside the ruins of the South Serene University. Bedraggled, exhausted, and suffering from a shortage of food because their trip had taken longer than they expected. They'd lost no one, not even a chicken.

Ethan Johnson greeted them. "My God, it's Emily Dickson!" He lifted her up and swung her around. "I think you've lost weight. Or maybe it's me. Maybe I'm stronger now." He set her back on the ground and the smile disappeared from his face. "But who are your friends, and where have you appeared from?" He stopped talking and shook his head. "No, no, none of that matters. You're here now and very welcome. Come and meet the others."

Epilogue

Keilani Alana celebrated her 100th birthday eighty years after nuclear and thermobaric bombs, electromagnetic pulses, and forest fires destroyed Neuvo Britannica. Of the population hunkered down in the ruins of South Serene University five years after the chaos, only Mia and Emma, small children when they arrived, were there to help her celebrate. Ethan, her husband for 60 years, had passed fifteen years earlier at eighty-three.

Hard work building a new community with only the most rudimentary tools, and the lingering effects of exposure to nuclear radiation, may have reduced the lifespans of some residents. Akari Yamada was the first to go, succumbing in her thirties to what everyone thought was the lingering effects of radiation. Many others lived into their sixties and seventies. Keilani came from a group of small Serene Sea islands near the equator where extreme longevity was the norm. She was in no hurry to join her ancestors.

University had grown from eight hardy survivors when she and Ethan arrived seventy-five years earlier. It now had a population of 524, including four generations of her large family.

They were still living in basements and even subbasements of the university buildings. Turbines in the East River now supplemented power from their aging nuclear reactor. In Uplands and elsewhere, turbines were the primary source of electrical power.

Life was good. They'd planted more fields with an increasing variety of fruits and vegetables. They had chickens, goats, and sheep, and workhorses to pull the plows they needed to keep their fields productive. Fish from the sea, lake, and rivers augmented the food they grew. Rabbits were abundant and easily killed.

Their community looked pretty strange. Just the tidied up remains of the glass and steel university buildings surrounded by various fields and paddocks separated by stone walls. In the absence of trees for wood-framed buildings or rocks they could shape into building blocks, building homes in the basements of university buildings seemed like their best choice. They repaired damaged parts of the ground floors, the ceilings of their underground abodes, with salvaged pieces of translucent plastic. Everyone spent most of the daylight hours outside, either in their fields or amongst the twisted steel posts on safe parts of the ground floors of the various buildings.

Bamboo they transplanted from the animal refuge near the hidden forest was propagating nicely. They'd already used the long, straight, and strong stems to make new farming tools and improvements to their underground abodes. They'd soon have enough bamboo for houses, like the one Emily Dickson built in the animal forest so many years earlier.

The only other substantial community, population nearing 400, was Uplands, the vacation resort in the foothills of the mountains in the west. Architects designed those buildings to withstand forest fires, and many survived the fires that swept across their entire island.

Once the denizens of University, with their friends from the hidden forest, eliminated the threat associated with fascists, the citizens of the mountain resort became part of an island population that now exceeded 1500. They lived in harmony with the other alphan communities and the elves, fairies, and gnomes in the hidden forest.

One curiosity was the mayor of Uplands. After the elves cleared the fascist rebels from the community, they installed Rory MacGregor, the presumed son of old Noah, the shepherd with a flock of sheep on the mountainside above the animal refuge, as mayor. After seventy years, he looked no older than he did on the day he accepted the job.

On the afternoon of her 100th birthday, Keilani, Emma, and Mia set off on Keilani's annual visit with Bristlebrink and Mildred. Five young children, including two of her great-great-grandchildren, accompanied them. None of the tykes had seen the hidden forest or a fairy. Faye and several other fairies, hidden as they always remained when they could, sped them along the way. Otherwise, they couldn't arrive at the very distant hidden forest an hour after they left University.

Faye and her friends appeared to shrieks of joy from the youngsters as Keilani's entourage approached the now familiar mountain wall that contained the portal to the hidden forest. Five fairies settled children on their backs and half loped and half flew through the passageway to their forest. Faye stayed back to close the portal and accompany Keilani, Emma, and Mia through the dark passages at a pace a centenarian alpha could manage.

Inside the forest, they went straight to Bristlebrink's gnomish house. Mildred was waiting outside with tea and cakes because gnomish houses are too small for alphas. The five youngsters scampered off with Emma and Mia in tow to explore the magical wonderland they suddenly found themselves in.

Melian, the leader of the hidden forest, joined Keilani, Faye, Bristlebrink, and Mildred. The conversation soon turned to conditions on other continents.

"Our continued communication with elves in hidden forests elsewhere suggests you won't find any Apexian communities like ours."

When Bristlebrink mentioned exploring the great unknown, Keilani replied, "we have small, outrider canoes for near-shore fishing. Be a long time before we have boats that can cross great expanses of ocean."

"But we could use outrider canoes with provisions for longer journeys," Bristlebrink said. "We could visit islands we know are to the north of us."

"Possible," Keilani replied. "And some of our fisherfolk have talked about it. But we don't have a seafaring tradition. And can't spare any fishers or their canoes."

"But that's your heritage. You may find communities that escaped the conflagration on those tiny atolls," Bristlebrink replied. "I'm surprised you're not more supportive."

Keilani shook her head. "Born and raised on an island far to the north and east. I'm just being practical. Let them come to us. I wish, however, we could erect signs inside our northern reef to warn any visitors of the danger from radioactive contamination."

Melian glanced at Faye, who nodded. "That we could do, and Eastport too. They should direct any overseas visitors to your fishing port."

On the way home, Keilani pondered their future. They were in an enviable position. The only place where technologically oriented alphas had learned to coexist with magical folk in the hidden forests. It was much more than mere coexistence. They were working together to produce a new world order, one that could survive for millennia. Would the five sleepy tykes riding home on the backs of fairies become leaders of that world?

The End

About the author:

Alan Kemister is the pen name of a Halifax Nova Scotia-based scientist experimenting with creative writing. He has a keen interest in environmental science and dabbled in yachting and golf before turning to fiction after retirement. He's written several dozen published short stories and one poem. Some of these appeared in four anthologies produced by Halifax's Evergreen Writers Group: *Out of the Mist: 22 Atlantic Canadian Ghost Stories* in 2014, *Off Highway: Journeys of Nova Scotia Writers*, in 2017, *Waters Edge: Prose and Poetry Celebrating Nova Scotia's Aquatic Heritage*, in 2020, and *Mystifying Moments: Stories and Poems by Nova Scotia Authors*, in 2024.

A Body in the Sacristy was Alan's first novel, and the first of the Barrettsport Mysteries featuring Detective Simon Goodyear and the fictional South Shore Nova Scotia town of Barrettsport. It was released in the spring of 2018. *Tilting at Windmills*, the second Barrettsport Mystery appeared later in 2018, and recently after a gap of six years when he worked on another project, he's released *The Body on Karli's Beach*, his third book in the series: https://www.amazon.ca/Body-Karlis-Beach-Alan-Kemister/dp/1775345998/

During those six lost years, he published a series of climate change novels culminating in *the Road to Environmental Armageddon*, a precautionary tale about the hazards of climate change denial. Here's the link to the paperback version: https://www.amazon.ca/Road-Environmental-Armageddon-Climate-Change/dp/177534598X/ *Starting Over Again* continues his interest in the climate change problem.

Other Links:

Email: alkemi47@gmail.com

Facebook: https://www.facebook.com/Phil.Yeats47

Website: https://alankemisterauthor.wordpress.com

A Body in the Sacristy: https://books2read.com/u/bMxDPk

Tilting at Windmills: https://book2read.com/u/3RzynB

The Souring Seas: https://books2read.com/u/mlEv29

Building Houses of Cards: https://books2read.com/u/bWEQox

They All Come Tumbling Down: https://books2read/u/meXjVR

www.ingramcontent.com/pod-product-compliance
Lightning Source LLC
Chambersburg PA
CBHW070523130626
46555CB00003B/1316